For Colin

GEMSTONE

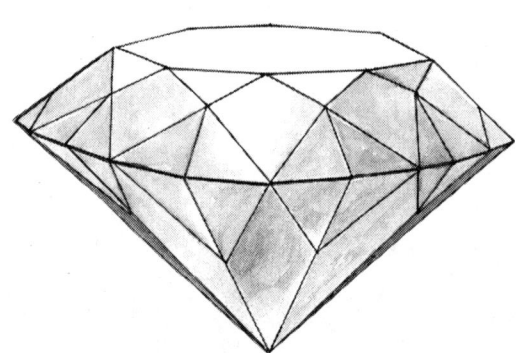

AND OTHER FATEFUL TALES

by

John Margeryson Lord

Order this book online at www.trafford.com/07-1795
or email orders@trafford.com

Most Trafford titles are also available at major online book retailers.

© Copyright 2008 John Margeryson Lord.
All rights reserved. No part of this publication may be reproduced, stored in a retrieval system, or transmitted, in any form or by any means, electronic, mechanical, photocopying, recording, or otherwise, without the written prior permission of the author.

Note for Librarians: A cataloguing record for this book is available from Library and Archives Canada at www.collectionscanada.ca/amicus/index-e.html

Printed in Victoria, BC, Canada.

ISBN: 978-1-4251-4300-8

We at Trafford believe that it is the responsibility of us all, as both individuals and corporations, to make choices that are environmentally and socially sound. You, in turn, are supporting this responsible conduct each time you purchase a Trafford book, or make use of our publishing services. To find out how you are helping, please visit www.trafford.com/responsiblepublishing.html

Our mission is to efficiently provide the world's finest, most comprehensive book publishing service, enabling every author to experience success. To find out how to publish your book, your way, and have it available worldwide, visit us online at www.trafford.com/10510

 www.trafford.com

North America & international
toll-free: 1 888 232 4444 (USA & Canada)
phone: 250 383 6864 ♦ fax: 250 383 6804 ♦ email: info@trafford.com

The United Kingdom & Europe
phone: +44 (0)1865 722 113 ♦ local rate: 0845 230 9601
facsimile: +44 (0)1865 722 868 ♦ email: info.uk@trafford.com

10 9 8 7 6 5 4 3 2

Notes:

All the characters in these stories are purely imaginary, and any resemblance to any person living or dead is unintended.

By the same author–

THE TRAP And Other Fateful Tales

SNOW QUEEN And Other Fateful Tales

DEDICATION

This book is dedicated to all my good friends who have given me nothing but encouragement and advice, and in a couple of instances have put up with my reading every single story to them as a try-out, and even mostly managed to stay awake.

And my special thanks to Ivy who proof read for me, spotting all those errors I'm certain I never made.

Thank you all.

ACKNOWLEDGEMENT

To Richard Brinsley Sheridan (1751 - 1816), for Mrs Malaprop who's idiosyncratic use of words I have borrowed for `In A Word'; although my Marion Spink would no doubt say `that she is quite enabled to specify her vocalities for herself, thank you very much.'

CONTENTS

THE MAN WHO MADE MONEY 11
WHAT'S GOOD FOR ONE 23
SELFFE V SELFFE.. 33
THE TIME TRAVELLER 43
IN THE EYE OF THE BEHOLDER 51
DEATH BY MACHINE 57
IN A WORD 73
THE SOUND OF BRASS 81
GEMSTONE 89
CHAIN REACTION 97
THE UNDERSTANDING... 109
FAITH 119
THE WARNING 131
CHARITY.. 143
THE STALKER.. 151
HOPE 161
INVASION 169
THE MAN WHO DUG... 179
MURDER - THE ONLY SALVATION 189
THE WAY THAT MONEY GOES ROUND.................197

⋞ **THE MAN WHO MADE MONEY** ⋟

*L*eslie (Les) Simpson Donaldson seemed a very ordinary fellow - but that is just what he was not.

Underneath his ordinariness he was extremely wealthy, at least his wife Lucy and three grown sons William, George, and Sam, assumed he was. It appeared that they could ask him for almost any amount of money and in due course it would be forthcoming; although larger sums took longer to arrive than smaller ones.

The source of this wealth was unknown as Les did not work and as far as anyone knew he had not inherited anything of significance. That was at least when the lads were small, but as they grew into young adults, each with a university education, suspicions grew in their home as to Les's secret.

To begin with there was the fortress. Les had built an extension to their very ordinary detached house which, to say the least, was unusual in its construction. The walls were of one foot thick reinforced concrete. Its door, the only one, had the look of wood but its heart was nine inch thick steel plate. It had two locks a combination and a very special key. It had a single large window which was of one-way glass making it possible to see out but not in.

Les's family had watched as he had installed one of the most professional and sophisticated telephone and computer systems anyone had ever established in a domestic environment. This extension even had its own address to which all Les's weighty correspondence was delivered.

And Les spent a great deal of time in `The Fort' as it became known.

It soon became obvious to his wife and sons that The Fort was somehow linked to the source of Les's ever ready cash.

As his boys grew Les realized that word of all this might leak out so he held a family conference where he gave them some hint about what he was up to, and a stern warning that if ever they told anyone else the funding to which they had all become accustomed would immediately cease. This dire statement had the desired effect and the secret of The Fort remained in the family. He also insisted that they lived well but not extravagantly so as not to arouse suspicion.

The family recognized the wisdom of maintaining secrecy and readily complied - just as long as the money came in it was OK with them.

Nevertheless, as an additional precaution, Les had given them the very barest of hints as to what he was about when ensconced in The Fort, whilst outside he was a very normal husband and father. He loved fun and spent many happy days playing soccer for the local old men's football team and was not a bad striker on occasion. The local pub would often find him amongst many friends clutching his pint and always ready to enjoy or tell a good joke.

A grammar school education had earned him a university place where he developed a fascination for higher mathematics in which he took his degree. It was this interest in mathematics which first started him off developing his own programs on his first decent sized computer. His interest evolved, and so gripped him that it was some surprise to himself as well as to others that he found the desirable Lucy and married her - or at least she found him - in fact she found him attractively built with readily smiling features and a good sound physique, and landed him before anyone else did.

Make no mistake, Les was no dried-up boffin, he loved his cuddly pleasure seeking Lucy, and for him there was no one else. And they were happy.

But then - there was The Fort standing as it did as a contrast to normal life. An object of strangeness and of isolation. Both an asset and a problem.

Whilst at university Les had inherited a small amount of capital from his late father which was mostly invested in the stock market in three or four medium sized companies. At first he had little spare time to devote to managing this resource and was content to simply spend the regular dividends as they occurred. But then, with his degree behind him he started to take a keen interest in these firms, their structure and their management philosophy. Soon this interest expanded to include several other businesses whose shares were quoted on the international stock exchanges.

It was then that he had his big idea.

Why not combine his mathematical know-how with his growing knowledge of the stock markets.

His first step was to compile a massive dossier on each of the two hundred or so companies which seemed currently to be stable and performing well. Next he analysed all aspects of these firms and began to give mathematical structures to them. Eventually after many hundreds of hours of concentrated work he linked these together in one massive algorithm.

Now, in order to run this enormous program Les had to use some of his inheritance to purchase and install a larger than normal computer system. In doing this he ran a portion of the formula on a small machine and used the results to liquidize the necessary shares, and to his surprise and encouragement the results worked out perfectly - he did well, beating the market pundits by a wide margin. The program worked - it was an auspicious beginning.

He was now married with three small children and a house supported by his university job as a lecturer in mathematics.

Pressure on his limited financial resources gave Les the push to go all out with his new algorithm for real, and this he now did.

It was a limited success. Run on a small system the program took too long to run.

He made money but realized that he could do much better with a much bigger system. That is when The Fort got built.

Secrecy was paramount, no one must even begin to guess that he had a way of capitalizing on the stock market and winning every time. It was time consuming and very hard work. He had to keep his list of information on every company on his file bang up to date all the time - but after discussing it with Lucy, he gave up his job and devoted himself to The Fort.

And so they did well. The lads grew up and had almost anything they needed, all provided from Les's stock market dealings. The algorithm seemed never to fail.

But - it was too good to last.

The fates grinned and took a hand.

Les collapsed whilst playing football one day shortly after his sixtieth birthday.

He was rushed to hospital where he just had time to whisper the code for The Fort to Lucy, tell her where the key was hidden, and swear her to secrecy, before he died of a severe heart attack.

There was no will, and so Lucy inherited everything - including The Fort and all its secrets.

At first they did nothing, but soon financial pressures began to make themselves felt and there was no Les to supply every need. So a family conference was held.

By now all three lads had finished at university and were considering some kind of employment, but the knowledge of what The Fort might provide both drew and intrigued them. Its secrecy promised vast rewards.

'At last, we will be able to make as much money as we want - we'll be rich,' was young Sam's view. 'All we have to do is to do what Dad did only more so.' The thought filled him with excitement.

'But we have no idea how it's done,' cautioned the older, wiser, William.

'We have to try,' was the middle man George's considered view.

In fact they were all secretly excited by the dream of unlimited cash, and eager to go ahead as fast as possible. Sam couldn't sleep for dreaming about being rich, he felt he might then have some chance with that posh girl he had more than his eye on.

George dreamed of a fast and sleek sports car, whilst William would settle for what they had before.

They had by now understood that their father had developed a mathematical formula for predicting financial advantages when dealing on the stock markets; and all this was available in The Fort.

It was agreed that they should keep it to themselves.

William had shown some ability in mathematics so it was agreed that he should be nominally in charge, and one fine day about six months after the funeral they all stood feeling slightly guilty but gripped by excitement outside The Fort's big door. Lucy supplied the code and they heard the reassuring thud of a bolt being electrically withdrawn. The big key was produced and turned in the lock. William took hold of the handle and pulled, and the door swung open.

William was the first to enter, and what he saw he would never forget.

`Good God Almighty,' was all he could utter as he stood fixed in amazement in the doorway.

The others pushed their way in and stood silent in awe.

The whole room was immaculately tidy and it had a very business-like look. It had the hallmark of a professional environment.

Below the one large window was a big desk its surface neatly arranged with a speaker telephone and the usual office paraphernalia, but mostly devoted to a giant computer screen. One wall was completely taken up with a stack of computer equipment and associated cabling. The remaining wall floor to ceiling had shelves stacked with files clearly labelled, colour coded, and stacked as formally as everything else in that unique place. As they stood there stunned into silence it felt as if The Fort had an atmosphere about it that was almost religious. It seemed to demand reverence.

Not knowing what to do with their find they agreed to touch nothing but that William would have the entry code and key, and he would without changing anything try to assess their ability to use The Fort and its contents as their father had done to their mutual advantage. He was also charged with the job of trying to understand the mathematics, whilst George was given the task of studying and keeping up to date the library of information on the companies involved. Sam was asked to gain a working knowledge of the large computer system.

Thus `The Team' as they called themselves, decided on a period of one month to familiarise themselves with the workings of The Fort, after which they would conduct a trial run using real and up to date information and real companies. However in this dummy trial they would not place real buying and selling instruction or use real money, the idea being to assess the results without entertaining any financial risk.

They did well to develop a sound understanding of how the system worked, but the result was puzzling especially to William, who, having carefully studied the closely guarded and secret mathematical model had come to the conclusion that its results were no better than those achievable by mere guesswork.

Despair set in, but they decided on the trial anyway.

`We need to prove it one way or another, and preferably without risk,' was William's verdict.

A very sensible decision - readily agreed by the rest of the team and Lucy, who was now getting anxious about her lack of income.

So the day came for the trial.

Tense with anticipation the lads and Lucy crowded into The Fort.

George selected the companies to be involved from the massive library. Sam got the equipment up and running, whilst William input the data, set the time limit of seven days and started the run.

The program terminated after a tense hour, and the results stating what to buy and what to sell spewed out of the printer - a pause - and then finally a further single sheet of results appeared.

William whipped the paper off the machine, read it briefly, and gave a whoop of joy.

`It predicts a profit of two hundred and fifty percent on an investment of five thousand pounds,' he said. `It seems we're in the money.'

Every one in that room breathed a sigh of relief. It seemed that not only were they saved from poverty at a stroke but that their dreams were about to come true. All they had to do now was to wait the seven days before checking the actual result with that predicted by the program.

It was all systems go, and there was a gleeful atmosphere about the Donaldson household.

But - could it really be that easy?

As each day passed William became more concerned.

He checked the market figures at each day's closing and noted that the program predictions were not being carried out in reality. What was even worse was that they were significantly poorer. This bad news he kept to himself.

At the end of the seventh day William entered an expectant room with a sheet of paper in his hand and faced four grinning faces, and his heart sank.

'I'm sorry,' he said. 'I have here the results and I'm afraid it's not good news. In fact it's bloody awful news.'

He paused, and wished he was somewhere else.

'Well come on then tell us the worst,' said Sam with a sinking heart.

'Not only did the real market not give us our calculated profit, but -' he paused, 'there was even a small loss of some five hundred and ten pounds.'

He was greeted by a stunned silence.

'What the blazes did we do wrong?' George asked eventually.

'Sadly - nothing,' William replied quietly.

'What do you mean - nothing,' Lucy asked. 'Les made it work so why can't we?'

She was very close to tears.

'I have been concerned for some time now that Dad's program just did not work, his success was probably due to the know-how he gained from his vast library of information stored on those shelves full of files gathered painstakingly over many years,' William told them.

'No,' shouted George. 'You're just telling us that because you want it all to yourself.'

He was furious.

William was patient. 'That's obviously wrong, since if the system worked there would be ample for all of us.'

'And it was a damn good job we didn't use real money,' he added.

George saw the sense of this and quietened down. 'So, what now he asked?'

'Let's at least do a few more dummy runs just to be sure,' Sam offered quietly.

And so it was agreed.

One month and seven dummy runs later the results were in and were disastrous.

Six showed a loss with only one demonstrating a very modest gain, and even this was due to an unexpected bid for a company which surprised the market.

A family meeting was called and it was decided to abandon The Fort, and they would all apply for jobs, including Lucy. Not everyone was unhappy about this - it seemed to be - 'more normal'.

They also agreed that The Fort and its contents should be destroyed, 'just in case'.

And so - one day the equipment was removed and smashed with a sledge hammer and a bonfire was made of the files and other documents.

It was a lovely balmy summer's evening as they stood around the last dying embers of the fire when suddenly William grabbed a stick and at some risk to himself managed to save a single charred page from the fire.

The words on it could just be made out - and aloud he read -

"I have come to realise that when the program is run as a trial without real money being invested it always fails. But it always succeeds when proper investment in line with its instructions is made.

This seems sensible since the real investment has an effect on the market and thus the ultimate result."

It was initialled - "LSD"

JML 4/12/2006

⊰ WHAT'S GOOD FOR ONE...... ⊱

They had, they both felt, been married too long. A terrible tedium had set in, and things were getting desperate. Both felt that they were approaching some limit beyond which lay dire consequences. Of this, they said nothing to each other, for fear of triggering some frightful irrecoverable conclusion.

Things might have been different had they had children, but early postponement for financial reasons led to a general reluctance to change the status quo and share their lives and time with the problems of growing offspring. They also both felt shy of the responsibility.

The stable routine of their lives lay about them like a protective cloak which they were all too used to, and too lazy to change.

After all it would mean giving up so much they had come to accept and enjoy, holidays abroad, meals out, party going, hobbies, would, they felt, have to be severely curtailed; that is judging by their friends with families.

Interestingly they never discussed the issue with each other, they merely assumed that the other felt the same way. Which was largely true.

However this self-centered life style was now, in their thirtieth year of marriage, posing something of a problem. This was largely because neither of them had developed any absorbing or creative interests. They hadn't even tried.

This was not due to any lack on the part of either, rather it was because there was never any pressure to make the necessary effort.

Until now.

Paul had done well in business reaching the dizzy height of general manager for a successful local firm, and this had enabled him to retire early at the age of fifty-five and still be very comfortably off. Whilst he had very much looked forward to being at home, June, his wife was not so sure.

Their lives forced into this permanently close and intimate environment soon became day long periods of irritation. Paul had nothing to occupy him, whilst June wanted the return of her previous freedom.

Now this was a shame because up to now they had enjoyed their life together in spite of its lack of excitement, and in spite of a love life that had slowly diminished from acceptable to infrequent and latterly to non existent. In fact Paul gradually came to the conclusion that his wife did not enjoy the experience over much. June frowned on risqué jokes and regarded with disapproval innuendo on television. Separate bedrooms had long been the order of the day. The subject of sex was simply never discussed.

This was very sad indeed since they were still both attractive individuals, the world having been kind to them, and possibly due to their not having had children.

They had met at fifteen, and were the same age, their birthdays being within a few days of each other, had fallen in love and were married at twenty. So it had been a long time.

Paul still admired his June, tall, she was an elegant dresser assisted by her slim but appropriately proportioned figure. Blonde curly hair graced a pleasing face lit by a pair of laughing blue eyes and smiling lips. By the standards of most male acquaintances she was `a looker', and she even had her admirers. And judging by the reaction of most females who met him, Paul's lean yet muscular frame and masculine features were equally attractive.

But these two were all too used to each other.

The magic had completely gone.

They no longer thought of each other in a sexual context.

They had too much time on their hands and the days seemed to both to be endless.

Paul tried some basic DIY but after a disaster with a shelf he attempted to fit and an emergency call to an electrician when he `fixed' a light fitting - June stopped him doing any more damage.

Then they began to fall out. Mere bickering became angry words. Angry words became periods of stony silence. Eventually they both threatened to leave. But as neither had the courage to take this step they decided something just had to be done before the situation became lethal. And so, belatedly they held a no holds barred discussion.

The breakfast table was cleared and they sat regarding each other gloomily across the table - neither wanted this and neither wanted the first say.

After what seemed a long time June gave a sigh and began -

'Well, this can't go on much longer,' she said. 'you are driving me mad.'

'Why? I don't do anything.' Paul was puzzled.

'That's the whole problem,' rejoined June. 'You don't.' This said with feeling.

'You'r always damn-well there doing absolutely nothing, and always in the way - that's just it you're always in the way.'

Paul was silent and unhappy, not knowing what on earth to say in response to what he recognised as nothing short of the truth. She had stated it as it was.

'You'll have to find something that takes you out, out of the house and away from being constantly under my feet.' This said with some bitterness.

Paul was silent, then - a plaintive plea, 'But what?' He had no idea, and what was worse no idea how to go about it.

June's reply was uncompromising. 'I have not the faintest notion, but other people manage it, and it had better be soon.'

Then more friendly. 'Why not take up some hobby or interest which will take you out and occupy you - not something like computing where you will still be here getting in my way. Something like bird watching or golf? Ask around at the pub.'

The sense of this got through to Paul, and he agreed to try.

And he did.

He joined the local U3A - the University of the Third Age. A group of people who were mostly retired and who gathered together to organise groups with common interests. The local branch had groups for nearly everything you could think of - from swimming, walking, reading, music and so on. There was even a water divining group. They made Paul welcome and he liked the friendly atmosphere and its relaxed do as you please approach - you could do as much or as little as you wanted to. And with June's admonishment in mind he joined the casual walking group whose policy was a short walk, lunch at a pub and a stroll back to the cars, and the naturalist group with its walks and lectures.

***

June was delighted.

They seemed to have found the answer to the problem of living together, but little did they realise the trauma this would bring to their lives.

Paul took to the new regime, and was secretly pleased that both his groups had a preponderance of ladies who showed a real interest in him as the only good looking male. He was considerably flattered by their attentions, and soon began to enjoy and look forward to the outings.

June was delighted and domestic peace returned.

But much suppressed desires were about to make themselves felt and freedom was about to bite.

A gorgeous younger girl joined the naturalist group.

The first thing anyone noticed about Karen was her sexual vitality, in some indifinable way her very feminine figure advertised it. Then her long reddish-brown hair, sensual eyes and mouth enhanced it. Strong men became tongue tied when they met her. But she was knowledgeable and was happy to share her learning with our Paul who found himself drawn to her. They naturally found themselves on the walks stopping often to inspect some flower, heads together, as Karen explained the finer points of identification. They would then run laughing to catch up with the rest of the group.

It happened quite naturally.

On one of these walks they had fallen far behind the main body when it turned to rain - the skies suddenly opened and it came down in buckets. Paul lent Karen his coat and they ran for shelter under the roof of a nearby barn. The rain had made them cold and Karen quite naturally snuggled up to Paul for warmth.

Poor Paul, he had no chance. It had been such a very long time since he had been this close to a woman, and a beautiful nubile one at that.

He kissed her.

She gave him a quizzical look and kissed him back and in a way he had never been kissed before. As the rain hammered on the barn roof they made urgent love there and then in the loose hay piled on the floor. Afterwards they lay for a long time just holding each other not saying a word and then made love again very slowly and with great tenderness.

He told her he loved her, and he meant it. The realisation had been long in coming, but he now knew he had fallen deeply under her spell. For the first time in years he felt he was a man, and his heart leapt and soared.

After this they met regularly at an hotel in a nearby but out of the way village and their relationship became a thing of permanence. She told him nothing about her situation, without a ring he assumed her to be unmarried and he let her believe that he was also on his own. In spite of this however it was clear that both preferred to keep their affair secret.

At home all was peaceful.

Then Paul, not usually very observant, began to notice things. His wife began to look extraordinarily cheerful. He thought he caught an occasional look of guilt on her returning home after some outing or other, and he became aware that she prepared and dressed with unusual care on these occasions. But the guilt of his affair prevented his ever mentioning the change in June which was becoming more obvious day by day.

He knew now that she was also having an affair.

Hurt and jealous at first Paul realized that he was powerless to intervene without risking his own wrong doing, about which he wondered if June had guessed, even as he had about her.

As he observed his wife's obvious new found pleasure with life he found it hard to accept that she had found a man who had the ability to engender this joy in her.

Married life continued in this artificially friendly atmosphere for several months.

Then as they were arranging their next meeting Karen told Paul she would be away for a month - `visiting a sick friend' she said. But she would make up for it next time, and they arranged to meet in a different place when she returned, and they fixed the date and time.

Paul was disappointed but felt he had no choice but to put his desires on temporary hold. Anyway, he thought he could do with a rest from the emotional turmoil he found himself in.

During this break Paul returned to going on U3A walks and tried to assuage his longing for the passionate Karen.

Anyway life at home was pleasant with June now a very different person. He caught her in unguarded moments with a very secret smile lighting her handsome features, and he wondered what her chap was like. Was he younger, more handsome, richer, would she leave home to join him? He did his best to dismiss these thoughts.

***

Then came the day of Karen's return.

They had arranged to meet at noon at a local but quiet hotel, and Paul was there early, eager and somewhat nervous in anticipation. His heart was misbehaving badly and he ordered a large whisky to calm himself.

Noon came and went without any sign of Karen, and Paul's nervousness was exacerbated by anxiety, he couldn't stop glancing from his watch to the door. He ordered another drink and took it to a table in the corner from which he would be certain to see her as soon as she arrived - if she arrived.

He saw them both at the same time, he couldn't help it, they entered arm in arm smiling into each other's eyes, clearly and without doubt deeply in love.

So absorbed in one another were they that he had time to see clearly from the way they held each other that their obvious passion was achingly physical.

His wife saw him first and stopped dead.

Then lovely Karen looked to where she was staring and also saw him, and gaped white faced.

She had got her dates mixed up.

She had also not associated the two - after all Brown was a common enough surname, wasn't it?

No one moved or spoke as the emotionally charged atmosphere held them in its grip.

From this moment on life for all three would be very different.

***

JML
9/12/2006

⸙ SELFFE V SELFFE ⸘

*J*ohannus Selffe, he pronounced it with a `y`as in Yohannus, thought of himself as an author, and he invariably referred to himself as such when ever the conversation allowed. It was either that or as a writer.

True, he had seen his work published, a fact of which he was still enormously proud although it was some nine years ago. He was now thirty and had seen nothing of his in print since then, which was not for want of trying.

The Work entitled `A Bird In The Hand' was a factual tale of how he had rescued an injured blackbird, taken it to the vet, persuaded them to tend to it, and in due course returned it to the wild, or at least his garden. The story went on to describe how he knew which bird it was due to its having a small white patch on each wing, and how it stayed in his garden for several subsequent years and came to feed from his hand.

This very short article had been accepted and printed in a popular women's magazine `Housewife' which had found itself with a lack of the usual contributions.

Johannus held down a small job at the local megastore doing odd jobs and `go-fetch- carrying' for other staff members as required.

He was a tall, fit and handsome chap, with a shock of crisp curly hair and a ready smile. He was always helpful and polite which made him popular with staff and customers alike, in fact many an elderly lady would stop and make quite a fuss of him - never failing to ask how his writing was going.

'How is the latest work coming on?' He would be asked.

'Quite well, thank you, I have about another ten pages to do before it's finished,' he might reply. Or - 'I'm stuck at the moment - waiting for inspiration.'

In fact he had not completed a single piece, long or short, since that first attempt, although many unfinished manuscripts lay about.

And Johannus was unlikely to get any farther as an author.

You see Benjimine would get in the way.

Benjimine Selffe was also a would-be writer and was permanently critical of everything Johannus attempted. But Benjimine had never had anything published.

These two rivals had much in common. They both lived with a fairly well-to-do mother who looked after them, and their very comfortable accommodation. But whereas Johannus went out to work Bejimine had no job to occupy him, and this gave him much more time for his writing.

Jealousy was the order of the day between these two, and their dislike of each other was ever present in both minds.

This situation was unstable to say the least.

Under the otherwise placid nature of Johannus a volcano was brewing. When it erupted it would involve many bystanders and even the law.

The beginning was quite unspectacular.

One day at work a customer showed Johannus a copy of the latest 'Wonder House' magazine in which was a short article which, she said, reminded her of Johannus's own story in that early edition of 'Housewife'. But the author was clearly stated as being Benjimine Selffe.

Johannus was beside himself with anger. Speechless with fury he waved his arms about and started to hurl the shop goods about. A tin of beans hit a neatly stacked pyramid of bargain tins of dog food which promptly collapsed and tins rolled everywhere getting under feet and setting off a chain reaction downing other stacks of goods. A full jar of jam landed by a till and promptly spread its contents far and wide. Johannus was fortunately stopped by the intervention of the store security man just as he was about to hurl a full bottle of champagne across the line of checkouts. Luckily no-one was injured and slowly staff and customers came out of hiding as Johannus was led away.

As Johannus was escorted from the floor still clutching the offending magazine he was heard to shout -

'That bloody Benjimine, I'll kill him. I really and truly will. The thieving swine.'

Things now began to get serious.

Johannus now had lost his job and had too much time on his hands.

He knew by heart the precise wording of the earlier article and had no need to check that the new one by Benjimine was word for word identical.

His long term hatred of Benjimine now boiled over and he became determined to smash him once and for all. It became his sole purpose in life - his other writing was put aside.

He had read that plagiarism, which is what this clearly was, was against the law, and so determined to bring the full weight of the legal system down on Benjimine's head.

Thus the next day Wolf, Thorpe and Badger solicitors found Johannus at their reception desk asking for an appointment to see a solicitor. Johannus wanted the best so he picked a well established city firm.

He had saved quite a bit from his wages and was able to convince them that he was serious and they arranged for him to meet the young Mr. Badger the following week.

He ignored his mother's concerned attempts to dissuade him and spent the time preparing his case, which he considered to be watertight. He made copious notes and had copies of both articles printed and underlined, in each, the sentences and phrases that Bejimine could only have copied.

He had soon compiled quite a dossier of evidence.

As he proceeded he became increasingly certain that in a court of law he would win and began to consider what amount of damages he would claim from the detestable Benjimine. He considered that it should be enough to convince Benjimine never to attempt to commit such despicable act ever again. Eventually and after much thought he decided that the sum of ten thousand pounds would just about be enough.

The day of his appointment came, and Johannus arrived at the solicitors, and firmly clutching his thick folder of evidence was promptly shown into the office of the young

Mr. Michael Badger.

Mr. Badger stood as Johannus entered, held out his hand, and said, 'How do you do? Mr. Johannus Selffe? I'm Michael Badger, do please take a seat.'

Johannus sat and gazed around him. He had never been in a solicitor's office before and was impressed by the quantity of paper and files lying about. His attention was drawn back to the job in hand by Michael saying, 'Well then what have you come to see us about?'

'Plagiarism,' said Johannus and stopped.

'Do go on,' responded Michael. 'Please tell me all about it.'

This should be good, he thought. He wasn't sure if Johannus was serious. In any case they had never had one of these before, it made a change from building conveyancing. He might have to delve into the law books. And mentally he rubbed his hands at the prospect.

Johannus opened his folder and spread the relevant pages before Michael, bringing his attention to the two magazines with what he claimed to be identical articles. He pointed at the author's names and the published dates, ensuring that Michael understood that his, Johannus's, was the earlier of the two.

The room was silent as Michael examined the papers, then put his hands together in deep thought unsure what to do next.

He made up his mind.

'Well you do seem to have a good case. I see you are asking for ten thousand pounds in damages. I need to discuss this with my partners before we can advise you. Can you leave these documents with me and I'll be in touch as soon as we have come to a decision?'

Johannus agreed, thanked him, and left.

A week or so passed before Johannus heard from his solicitors, and then it was not as he had expected.

He was asked by letter to make an appointment, which he promptly did.

This time there was Mr. Michael Badger and Mr. Thomas Thorpe, a much older man and clearly senior, sitting opposite him. It was he who spoke first after the introductions.

'Well now,' he started. 'We have received a letter from Messrs Will and Pound solicitors. Not to put too fine a point on it - it is a counter-claim on behalf of a Mr. Benjimine Selffe, also for ten thousand pounds in damages.' He paused. 'Tell me is he a relation of yours?'

Johannus appeared stunned, and did not reply to the question.

'Tell me,' he said. 'On what basis does he make his claim?'

'He says that he can produce a draft version of the same article which pre-dates your earlier magazine date by a good twelve months,' the senior man replied.

Johannus swore.

'So! What now?' He said.

Mr Thomas drew a deep breath well aware that they were somewhat out of their depth and feeling their way through a difficult and painful case.

'Without your detailed instructions we have taken the liberty of contacting Will and Pound,' he began. 'In summary we feel that it would not be in your or the other party's interest to go through the courts with the expense that this would entail. Instead we recommend that you agree to a meeting where the whole matter can be dealt with to everyone's satisfaction.' And will prevent our making fools of ourselves in public, he thought.

Johannus looked unhappy, but then said, 'Just as long as you are on my side, then OK.'

In due course the big meeting date and time was set, the venue being at Johannus's solicitors.

***

The big day arrived and Mr. Thomas and Mr. Michael of Wolf, Thorpe and Badger together with a lady short-hand typist sat in their big meeting room awaiting the arrival of their client Johannus Selffe and his opponent Benjimine Selffe with his solicitors Messrs Will and Pound. They were considerably on edge as they felt that this could go badly. All possible options had been explored but they were unsure of the legal status of some of the possibilities. It was all new territory for everyone.

But what happened in the end none of them would have predicted.

The time of the meeting arrived. There was a knock on the door and the receptionist stood there looking puzzled.

'Mr. Will and Mr. Pound,' she said, then after hesitating, 'and their client Mr. Benjimine Selffe.'

They entered, and Mr. Thomas cut the greetings -

'What the devil are you doing with our client?' He managed. Then - 'Are you or are you not Johannus Selffe?'

In a voice rougher and deeper than Johannus's, 'No I'm Benjimine.'

'Do you know where Johannus is?' he was asked.

Then in the voice with which his team was familiar Benjimine said 'I'm here of course.'

For quite some time no one said a word.

Mr. Thomas was the first to gather his wits and turning to Johannus/Benjimine asked him/them to go for a cup of tea with the secretary whilst they held a short conference, to which he/they agreed and they left the room.

You can imagine the questions that were raised and left unanswered. It was clear that their mutual client was suffering from some psychiatric condition which none of them had any idea how to deal with.

Credit where credit's due after an hour they invited Johannus/Benjimine back for their considered advise.

Again Mr. Thomas took control.

'We have considered both your claims thoroughly, and have concluded that both have some merit in law. In which case if it went to court it is probable that neither claim would win. Therefore we suggest most strongly that you both withdraw your claims and accept equal credit for the most excellent article as it appeared in both magazines.

Here he paused, but he was not yet finished.

'It has been a most stimulating case,' he went on, 'and if you agree to our proposal we have decided to waive all fees - in a word you owe us nothing.'

Johannus/Benjimine said nothing and the solicitors held their breath. Then with a show of reluctance agreed to the proposal, thanked them all in each voice in turn, first Johannus and then Benjimine, and left.

The secretary was sworn to secrecy and all present breathed a grateful sigh of relief.

JML
14/12/2006

PS - Multiple personality syndrome is a real and serious but fortunately rare psychiatric condition. It can be `helped' by qualified professionals. The story above is in no way intended to exploit those who may suffer from this problem.

Whilst the tale is purely fictional it is nevertheless based on genuine clinical data.

⁕ **THE TIME TRAVELLER** ⁂

*W*e, his friends, tried to distract him from his declared intentions, we really did. We introduced him to a phalanx of pretty girls most of whom would have been more than happy to occupy him. We gave big parties for him. We spent many long hours trying to change his mind. We even booked him on trips abroad with suitable female companions, which he cancelled.

But all this was to no avail.

He was desperately, totally, overwhelmingly in love. Whilst browsing through the 'Romance' section in the local library, he had read almost everything else, fate had directed his inquiring hand to a volume entitled 'Barbara Cartland's Book of Love and Lovers'. Curious, he flicked through its pages. It took just a single glance at the picture entitled 'Baigneuse Endormie' by the nineteenth century painter Theodore Chasseriau to captivate him. The model was Alice Ozy and her elegant nakedness and beautiful sleeping features charmed him. He became lost in a very personal dream there and then and had to be reminded where he was and that it was now closing time.

Tom Emit borrowed the book and spent the next few months finding as much as he could about the desirable mademoiselle Ozy. There was not much, but what there was, sent his heart racing. He learned that she died rich but alone and very lonely. This should never happen to such a lovely person he thought and badly yearned to do something about it.

And we believe he did, incredible though it seems.

Tom was no slouch. A powerful and active intellect had seen him obtain his masters degree in physics and astronomy. He was also a good all round sportsman, outstanding at rowing, rugby and tennis. Handsome and popular with both sexes he was always in demand for drinking sessions and dates.

He was also very, very rich. And we, his friends, actively protected him from would be leeches intent on exploiting his natural generosity.

And now here he was, lost in love for a person in a painting, a person long dead in fact. We were completely at a loss to know what to do.

Tom became a dull shadow of his former dynamic self, and took to studying the more advanced aspects of physics, gaining world-wide recognition for his papers on Quantum Theory and its practical applications in the modern world.

Now it is said that if you claim to understand quantum physics then you certainly don't, but Tom proved that he was an exception to the rule.

When quite suddenly all these conflicting ideas came together -

`I will build a time machine,' he declared, `and go back and find miss Ozy.'

`He's gone mad,' we said. `Bonkers, potty, doolally-tap.'

`We must stop him,' we declared.

And as I have said our every endeavour to do so ended in failure.

Tom knew that 'entangled' particles knew of each other's status no matter how far apart in the universe they were. He also knew that an electronic wave front could be made to travel faster than the speed of light. Such a wave could carry information, and he argued that if these two effects could be combined in some way then transportation in time might be possible.

Tom lived on his own in a large house that had been his parent's, and was looked after by a trusty 'daily woman'. He mostly ate out where he was a regular at the Griffin.

His first step in this madness was to clear everything out of the very large cellar, cover its walls with light plastic paneling, cover the floor with oak, and install positive pressure equipment to exclude any dust. He fitted out the space by the entrance as a dust free cloakroom where persons requiring entry could don dust free overalls, the wearing of which in the cellar was mandatory.

All this time we more or less lost him.

For the next six months he was fully occupied buying equipment most of which was to his own specification. All this he set up in the cellar and tested it.

Then suddenly, shockingly, he called us all together - to say farewell!

We were all assembled at the Griffin. Tom looking pale and somber, made sure we all had our drinks, called for quiet and began -

'My good friends,' he said. 'As you know I have been intent on going back into the past to meet the lady who has recently occupied my waking thoughts and my dreams. Should I succeed I shall be the happiest man on this planet,'

He paused. No one spoke.

'I expect to be away for about six months, and during this time it is imperative that the equipment in my cellar is not interfered with in any way.' He then announced the precise date of his expected return.

We, his friends, were stunned and very unhappy.

He then looked into each of our faces in turn.

'Do I have your word that you will ensure that this is the case?' He then asked.

Of course we all agreed, we had no choice.

Soon after this he said goodbye, and each of us in turn wished him God speed and before we could stop him, he left.

The atmosphere after he had departed was gloomy, the general consensus being that Tom had mentally slipped over the edge and we would be unlikely to see him again. Either that or his equipment, his time machine, would fail and he would turn up as usual the next day.

***

Tom did not turn up on the day following his announced departure, nor the next, or the next, or the next. If fact after a week we knew that he had gone. So according to our promise and in agreement with his house keeper we arranged a rota to go over and check that his cellar had not been tampered with. The door remained firmly locked the location of the key being only known to that trusty lady.

We put an ear to the door but all was as silent as the grave.

The only evidence of any activity was when the house keeper told them that the cellar had its own electricity supply and meter and she had, as instructed, just paid the bill for what seemed to her, and to us, a very high level of consumption. Whatever was in there it was using quite a bit of electrical power.

We concluded it must be his time machine perhaps running in stand-by mode ready for Tom's return.

This was clearly no joke. And we were worried for his safety.

And we had six months to wait.

Our little group was divided as to what to do for the best, and found ourselves divided into three broad camps.

One group, the smallest, was certain that we should advise the authorities, report Tom missing and break into the cellar where they thought they would find him either alive or dead.

A second slightly larger number thought that we should simply break in ourselves and discover what was going on.

The third and by far the largest group was for strictly observing our promise not to interfere for six months, at which time Tom would emerge from the cellar or they would deem their promise expired and then break in. In the end this view prevailed, and the sanctity of the cellar and its contents was strictly observed.

And for six months nothing changed.

***

The date of Tom's predicted return from the past arrived.

Our group of friends arrived in ones and twos at about dawn. The day was starting warm and sunny, promising to be hot later.

Tom's house keeper let us in and she and us crowded in and stood or sat outside the cellar door.

No one knew what to expect but all attention was on that door. I think we expected it to open with old Tom emerging. If not we were to ask the good lady for the key and enter, afraid to find Tom's dead body amongst a mass of machinery.

The situation was deadly serious. Six months ago Tom had entered this cellar and effectively locked himself in. Should they enter and find his corpse very serious questions would be asked.

Noon came and went, no one left apart from someone who was delegated to get some sandwiches and drinks.

A council of war was held and it was agreed that at midnight our promise would have run its course and we would enter.

Evening came and turned into night and our conversations ceased.

Night wore on, and we repeatedly looked at our watches or asked the time. Nerves were stretched taught. Someone started to weep quietly, and someone else cursed quietly calling Tom the worst kind of fool.

Midnight.

This was it.

The house keeper produced the key. It turned easily in the lock.

The door opened, but inside all was dark.

A light switch was found and the room was a blaze of light.

We crowded in.

What we saw was totally unexpected.

The room was devoid of anything that looked remotely like machinery apart from an air conditioning unit humming away by one wall. Three other walls were beautifully lit by a tasteful lighting system suspended from the ceiling. On these walls were hung a magnificent collection of paintings all of just one person - Alice Ozy. And we couldn't help but admire her breathtaking beauty.

The middle of the area was taken up with a comfortable settee and easy chairs and some elegant small tables. On one such table was a bottle of good port and a glass.

Eventually we found our voices, and everyone expressed surprise and wanted questions answered.

It was during this hullabaloo that someone came trotting down the stairs and stood smiling in the doorway.

`Hallo to you all,' said Tom. `Welcome to my little secret. Forgive me for keeping it from you but I thought you would think me mad.'

Everyone present was astonished but delighted to see the man standing all hail and looking very hearty, and in our hearts we forgave him.

I then asked `What about the time machine? And where have you been?'

We were quiet while he answered.

`Time travel, I believe to be impossible particularly into the past because of a stricture which proposes that if you go back in time and were to kill your grandparents you would then not exist to go back and kill them, clearly physically illogical. In fact, I never expected you to believe me. Where have I been? I've been in France to find out all I could about this lady.' He waved his arms at the pictures.

`I learned a great deal. Enough in fact to get her out of my system.'

At this we cheered.

`Now,' he said, `I've some bottles of good French wine outside and if someone will find some glasses I suggest we have a bit of a party, and if you wish I'll tell you all about Alice Ozy.'

A proposal to which no one objected.

JML
14/12/2006

◈ IN THE EYE OF THE BEHOLDER ◈

*Y*oung Arthur Pringle was not really young at all, he had always been called 'young' to distinguish him from his elder brother Andrew. At twenty two years old Young Arthur reckoned to know his own mind. Just two years ago he had fallen in love with Allison Makewait, and it was she he was determined to marry.

According to Arthur's friends and relatives this was a most unsuitable choice. Arthur was by the standards of most of the young ladies who came across him, and at his job in his father's successful butcher's shop there were plenty of these, he was an extremely attractive example of a marriageable male. Well built, tough, stern of aspect, and yet his striking features were always ready with a smile. The overall effect was one of reliable sincerity. And they all fell for him - in fact he could take his choice.

So then why the disapproval?

Well it's hard to say why without offending the young lady who was the source of his desires.

To say she was comely was probably understating the problem. Of Allison there was more than enough to go round.

'Why Allison?' His brother queried. From the knowledgeable position of two years of marriage and one lovely baby son he sought to advise his young sibling.

'You could have anyone, and there are some beauties about. What about Joyce - she's been after you for weeks, or Angela - her father is stinking rich?'

To which Arthur would merely shrug and protest that he loved Allison and it was his choice after all.

Allison and Arthur had grown-up together. Same junior school, and secondary school and same college where he studied butchery and business management and she did a course in domestic science. Ever since he recognized the sexual attraction of the opposite gender he was drawn to Allison.

So what could be the attraction?

Firstly like many a 'comely' person Allison was blessed with an easy going, happy nature. Her pleasantly rounded face was always ready to smile which she did often. She found life good and it showed. Make no mistake with lively grey-blue eyes, full red lips and short curly brown hair, Allison was very lovable. She made friends easily and was well liked.

But there were lots of girls with similar and better qualifications so why was Arthur hooked.

Well she turned him on. All the time and every time.

It had been two years earlier when they found themselves alone in his parent's house and had made love for the first time, and to say they were compatible was an understatement, they loved the experience and each other. And they became welded to each other, physically and emotionally.

Now whereas it was Allison's build that was a problem for others it was just this that made her special and sexually attractive to Arthur.

He loved her big soft breasts, adored her rich rounded thighs, and found her figure warm and welcoming - and all this he went for in a big way and wanted nothing more by way of a wife and lover. What's more she was a damn good cook.

Arthur despised the thin gaunt girls who were seemingly unable to relax and enjoy life for fear of putting on weight or not looking their best. They always seemed anxious and hard to please. He had been on dates with some of these who were generally considered by his mates as being 'cracking lookers' and had found them dull and self centered. Breasts that vanished when the owner lay down, waists that he could almost get two hands around, and legs that would make good broom handles were not for him.

As with his job he liked his meat to have plenty of flesh on it.

And why not.

But in this idyllic relationship a time bomb was ticking away.

They decided to marry.

Unfortunately this otherwise happy decision was the source of their undoing.

A date was chosen which was nine months or so ahead, plenty of time Allison considered to get herself organized.

She went to try on wedding dresses. And oh dear me!

The poor lass soon discovered that she was too ample to fit into any of the beautiful gowns, and those that would fit made her look matronly or merely 'frumpy'. The try-on was a disaster and Allison left in tears. After all she loved her Arthur and wanted to look perfect for him.

It was at this point that his well meaning brother decided to intervene for Arthur's sake and inadvertently sealed the tragedy.

He took Allison aside.

'I know Young Arthur loves you but if you want it to last perhaps you should try to loose a little weight?' This suggested by a man whose wife could hide behind a lamppost.

So Arthur soon found that Allison was unavailable for their usual meetings - she was at a slimming group. Or she was jogging. And when they went out for meals she would eat nothing.

She lost weight and looked thinner, but slimness didn't suit her. She looked gaunt and all angles with no round bits.

They made love less often and when they did it was a chore rather than a pleasure as Allison was always worrying about her looks.

Then they had a bust-up.

Arthur did not like this 'new' Allison and told her. He also told her the wedding was off and they were finished.

Sadly he neglected to tell her why.

Allison was desperately hurt, wounded and unhappy, left wondering what she could possibly have done wrong. She still loved her Arthur, and felt that she had done her best for him.

***

Arthur tried to find another Allison but all he girls he took out wanted to be thin.

GEMSTONE and other fateful tales

As for poor Allison herself she gave up ever finding another Arthur.

She also gave up her slimming group, and stopped worrying about her weight. Fond of her own excellent cooking she soon replaced the missing pounds she had spent such an effort to loose. Within the space of a few months the old Allison was back but without that inner joy her relationship with Arthur had given her.

Still popular, she was often asked out on dates.

The one glorious evening in summer Allison and a likable but not special boy arrived at an outdoor party. There was dancing and food and drink a-plenty.

Suddenly she spotted Arthur with a very elegant blonde girl.

He saw her - and from that moment he couldn't take his eyes off her - there was his old Allison looking soft and welcoming as ever she had been.

His heart raced and leaped in his breast and he could hardly breath.

He knew this was his one chance - it would not come again.

Allison lost sight of him.

Then as if in answer to some magic wish, there he was at her side. Ignoring the protests of her escort he took her hand and led her out into the night where without a word being spoken they made tender love then and there under the stars.

As she lay happily in his arms, he told her he loved her just the way she was. He said he didn't want a wedding but would she please consent to setting up home with him?

'I've seen just the place,' he said. 'I'm sure you will love it.'

Allison was too full to speak so she very simply kissed him.

Arthur had his answer.

JML
19/12/2006

⋐ **DEATH BY MACHINE** ⋑

It had been a long and arduous struggle. The task he had set himself had taken every waking minute of his life - he was now nearly sixty, and almost all of his considerable wealth. His bachelor status allowed him to devote all his attention to the project. But now at long last he felt he was very close to the end - and success.

William Walthemstow Wendle, or 'w cubed', as his close associates called him, was a world leader in automaton technology, specializing in creating machines that imitated human activities in the most realistic fashion.

His grand ambition was to create a machine in human form which was self reliant and could not be easily distinguished from the real thing.

Long ago he had built a computer which passed the Turing Test, ie. which when asked a question could not in its reply be distinguished from that of a real human.

And now here he was looking at the end product of all this work. There she stood looking truly beautiful - an android in human female form.

William's other passion was for old movies, and he would retire in the evening to his private cinema with a glass of good whisky and watch for the umpteenth time one of his old favorites. He knew most of them off by heart.

It was, therefore, no accident that his android took the form, mannerisms and voice of the most elegant and sexy of them all - Marilyn Monroe.

He wanted to bring her back to life.

And here at last on the 5th may 2056 stood the fully built result of all this work.

She was beautiful. Dressed in a clingy satin gown the sight of her made his heart pound - it was just as if Marilyn herself was standing there.

Now, whilst he had run all the appropriate tests on the separate parts of his creation he had as yet not switched on and let Marilyn do her own thing as she was programmed to do.

For this first run he had moved her out of the workshop and into the more environmentally suitable atmosphere of his very large and well appointed sitting room where he actually felt she would feel more relaxed. You see he had already started to think of her as having human-like feelings.

The curtains had been drawn for privacy and he had dismissed the technical and domestic staff and helpers. He was alone with his creation.

With the remote controller in his shaking hand and his finger on the 'go' button he hesitated. Desperately afraid something would go wrong and a lifetime's work be ruined, he went over every check again in his mind and could find no reason to hold back.

At first nothing happened. Marilyn did not move. Not even a blink of those big wide blue eyes.

William waited and began to wish he had someone with him, but secrecy was essential in case of failure.

But still there was no sign of movement. The only sound was the low hum of the air conditioning plant.

Then to his astonishment she slowly turned towards him and looking at him through lowered lids said in that sultry voice of Marilyn's that he knew so well -

'What's the matter big boy, aint you never seen a pretty girl before?'

He was so completely taken aback that without thinking what he was doing he answered her.

'Yes,' he said. 'But none as beautiful as you.'

'Well now isn't that a fine compliment, I think I'm going to like you big boy,' breathed Marilyn softly pouting those luscious lips and smiling.

'What do they call you? And where am I?' She added.

At this William was taken aback. All manner of things he had considered but sensible questions came as a surprise, so he tried to gain the initiative.

'I'm William, and this is my home, do please sit down and I'll answer any questions.'

At this Marilyn gently eased herself into the easy chair he had indicated, and looked across at him through half lowered lids.

This was not as he imagined it would be and to gain time to think he switched her off.

Later and with mature consideration he realized that such a close resemblance to Miss Monroe was a mistake, and so he decide then and there on some urgent modifications.

Marilyn's characteristics were eliminated from her programme, she was changed from a blond to a darkish brunette, and she was given an English accent.

A week later they were back in the sitting room and ready to begin again, and this time William had a script.

'On' - The girl awoke.

'Please sit down and kindly listen,' said William in a clear voice.

She sat, looked at him and waited.

William noted that although she was no longer Marilyn the lady opposite was just as sexually inviting. As she smiled at him William almost lost the thread of what they were about, and it was with considerable effort he brought himself back to the task in hand.

'You will now take note of all I am about to say and build it into your behaviour response system, and will act accordingly at all times.

'The name Marilyn Monroe is deleted, your name now is Mary Lynn,' he spelled it out, '- and you reside here at this address,' again he spelled it out.

'First and over-ruling principle - you will never cause harm, pain or injury to any human being - the detection criteria for humans is in your data bank.

'When your power system drops to the 25% level, or less, you must seek out a 13 Amp, 240 Volt, standard mains socket, plug yourself in and charge yourself to at least the 90% level.'

And so on. There were some two hundred guide rules which took several hours to finish.

GEMSTONE and other fateful tales

All through this Mary sat and nodded as each instruction was registered - as she was programmed to do. Then - 'Is that understood?'

'Yes,' said Mary. 'But if I am Mary Lynn, what are you called?'

William was taken aback. Here she was again asking a logical but unprovoked question. How did she do this? Her software was complex but as far as he knew this shouldn't be possible. It made him nervous, he didn't like unknowns, no engineer did.

There followed a further month of trials at the end of which William came to a natural point where he had nothing further to add. The rest he must leave to Mary's powerful built-in self-learning ability.

William got used to Mary's presence, it was like having a very pleasant and compliant partner - but for the never ending flood of questions - where on earth did they come from?

'Where did I come from?'
'You were built.'
'Who built me?'
'I did.'
'Who built you?'
'No-one, I was biologically conceived.'
'Are there others like me?'
'No. As far as I know you are unique.'
'Will you build others?'
'No, it would take many years and I will die before then.'
'Will I die?'

William hesitated. 'Er, no, but you may slowly wear out.'

'Will this take long?'

'Many years.'

'Oh!'

Now what was that all about, he wondered?

***

The appointed date for the press exposure was scheduled and was only a couple of weeks off when Mary disappeared from home.

***

A scruffy unemployed youth by the name of Anton Burke was wandering aimlessly down a dirty back street between tall brick factory walls and was trying to work out where the cash for his next fix was coming from. He was simply following his feet hoping something would turn up.

What he didn't know was that he didn't have long to live.

Turning the corner he found himself in a street full of shops and shoppers.

'Possibilities here,' he thought, and edged his way along.

Then he saw her.

His eyes bulged and his groin itched at the sight.

To his amazement the girl approached him.

'Excuse me,' she said. 'But I'm looking for somewhere to power up. Can you direct me please?'

He had no idea what she meant. All he knew was that she seemed vulnerable and this was an opportunity he wasn't about to miss.

'Yes, follow me,' he said.

And she did.

She had no bag, but that was usual round here, girls kept their cash in their shoes or elsewhere on their person.

It took just a few minutes for them to reach his squat, for him to push the door open, and invite her in. He tried the light switch and the bare bulb filled the entrance with a pale light. Someone had fixed the meter, it happened all the time.

He found himself trembling from head to foot.

'Upstairs,' he said pointing.

'OK, but first I need a standard thirteen-amp mains socket, I am at my lowest possible power level,' the girl explained.

Again he hadn't the remotest idea what she meant but there was a socket in the skirting on the next landing.

So. 'Upstairs,' he said again and followed her up.

She saw the socket and reached down with her modified first two fingers and thumb of her left hand intent on plugging in.

It was at this precise moment that, unable to restrain himself any longer, Anton made a lunge for her. Their bodies seemed tangled for a moment, but it was Anton who suddenly found himself off balance at the top of the stairs - tried to grab the banister rail, missed it, and fell.

His yell was cut short by the breaking of his scrawny neck and his lifeless body landed in an untidy heap on the lower landing.

The instant the girl plugged in, her system completely shut down until about four hours later when charging was complete. No-one entered the building in that time.

Charging completed, Mary's systems returned to life, she un-plugged herself and descended the stairs. On reaching the body her detectors surveyed it, and as it was now cold, her main human sensor being infra-red identified it as non-human, a mere bundle of rags in fact.

Mary left the premises and set off to find home using her built-in GPS system. But in this she was unsuccessful.

Anton's body was found later that night by a passing but curious penniless male by the name of Mead. Mead raised the alarm and the police were called.

***

Mary's body was found a couple of days later by the roadside about two miles from Anton's squat. She had run out of power. With no detectable life signs she was pronounced dead on arrival at the local hospital and transferred to the mortuary where she would be examined in due course by an overworked autopsy staff.

Bill Cooper, junior staff member was given the job of preparing the body for examination. He was puzzled and called his boss to come and look at something very strange. His boss Harry Scrine was annoyed at the interruption but strode across to look anyway, and what he saw puzzled him also. The lad was pointing at the girl's left hand where two fingers and her thumb were arranged so that the could be made to resemble a 13 Amp plug.

'What the hell have we got here?' He exclaimed. Although Harry appeared short tempered he was good at his job. He put down the knife he was holding and gave the body a thorough examination.

His conclusion surprised even him who claimed to have seen everything.

'We have here,' he announced eventually, 'what is known as an android - a made person. In fact a machine.'

Then to himself - 'I wonder?'

He then pulled over one of the rooms flexible mains extension leads, and after some hesitation he took the girls hand and plugged it in. Nothing happened but he noticed a tiny light was pulsing in her right side. Gently pulling back a flap of tissue he revealed a neat control panel which showed the charge level to be low.

'Well now,' he said. 'I think we will leave young missy here to charge up and then we will see what we've stumbled on. For now you must not speak to anyone about this on pain of losing your job.'

Much later that day they were both startled when the girl sat up, unplugged herself, swung herself off the table, and in a low but polite voice asked for her clothing.

Bill spilt his coffee and scalded his chest, Harry simply stood and gaped.

With her clothes on the girl looked normal and sat quietly answering their questions.

Then she asked to be allowed to return to the address she gave them, and they found her so beguiling that they simply put her in a taxi, paid the fare and saw her on her way.

It was only after she had gone that Harry realised he had a problem - the paper work. A dead person had been brought in and duly registered - and had then come to life and walked out again. It didn't happen all that often.

In the end he wrote it up just as it was. No-one read the reports anyway unless it was an important police case or person.

But this time - they did.

**

Events moved quickly.

William went to the police and reported Mary missing pretending she was his niece.

At the same mortuary Anton's body was identified and the cause of death - a broken neck - identified. He also had a high level of drugs in his system.

CCTV footage from outside Anton's squat was examined and the girl was seen entering the building with Anton and leaving four hours later alone.

The girl's picture was circulated, seen by Harry who then told the disbelieving police about his walking corpse.

The police called at William's, saw the girl and began an enquiry into a possible murder, insisting that Mary be switched off until further notice.

Forensic tests showed fibres of the girls clothing on Anton's, and his on hers.

The next thing that happened began a sensation which gripped the whole nation, everyone had a view and tempers ran high.

Anton's father turned up and insisted that his son had been murdered, by what he called that 'dreadful killing machine', and demanded compensation from its designer.

The press seized the golden opportunity.

Experts gave their opinions. Law cases were quoted. The uninformed ground their axes and the religious poured pious cold water on the whole blessed thing. But in the end it was left to the coroner's court to decide the true cause of Anton's death.

***

The date of the coroner's examination arrived, the small room was packed and the coroner's first act was to have everyone but the participants removed.

When he eventually had quiet he began.

'As far as I am aware, there are some aspects of this case for which there is currently no precedent. I therefore expect that following these proceedings it may be some time before I publish my findings.'

Justice Malcolm Breakshaft was an honest man who was determined that history would endorse what was to take place here and applaud his conclusion.

The first to be called was Mead who had discovered the body, but he was not to be found.

Next on the stand were the police.

The officer in charge related how they had been alerted to the finding of what he thought was a dead body by Mead. The scene was described, Anton was found to be dead and the police doctor and a forensic team called.

The doctor reported the time of death to be just after Anton and a girl were caught on CCTV entering the building. He stated that the position of, and injuries to, were consistent with a fall down a flight of stairs.

Then damningly he admitted that - no, he couldn't rule out foul play.

The forensic technician then told that he had found threads of the girls clothing on Anton and threads of his on hers.

He gave his opinion that they had been in close contact at some time.

CCTV footage was shown of the girl and Anton entering the building and of the girl leaving alone. The times were recorded on the tape.

Then came the sensation.

Harry Scrine was called and gave a vivid description of discovering that his corpse was not human but a beautifully built android. He also said he had found high levels of drugs in the body of Anton whose injuries were consistent with a fall down stairs, and no he couldn't rule out foul play.

This proved too much for Anton's father who stood up and pointing at William shouted -

`There you are you bastard, my boy was murdered by your bloody piece of machinery. How was he to know what she was. You will pay - I demand compensation. And that thing should be destroyed before it kills again.'

The court was in uproar. The coroner announced an adjournment until nine am the following day.

The press was full of it. Every angle was explored.

Attempted rape by Anton.

Attempted robbery.

Self defence by the girl.

Seduction by the girl.

Murder by the girl.

Murder by the girl's maker.

Irresponsibility in allowing the girl onto the streets.

How many more Mary Lynns were out there?

An accident.

The girl was a secret military weapon.

And inevitably - an invasion by aliens.

Anyway - why was the girl not in court to answer for herself.

Now this last point had been worrying the coroner, and he decided that the girl must appear to answer some of these questions, and perhaps tell the court what really took place. So before the end of that day he called William with his decision.

Reluctantly William agreed.

So, the following morning saw a full court buzzing with expectation.

Malcolm Breakshaft very much aware that the eyes of the public were on him, called for silence, and got it.

Into this silence the court usher spoke -

'Call Mary Lynn please.'

All eyes were on the door.

Mary strode confidently in, and a gasp of wonder and astonishment went up.

In walked a slim expensively but quietly dressed young lady of about twenty five. She was undeniably attractive, and had a strong but perfectly relaxed presence. Looking around curiously she was directed to the witness stand and asked to be seated, which she did.

William gripped the arms of his seat sick with apprehension - he had no idea what she would say or do.

At the sight of Mary, Anton's father lost control again, and pointing at her shouted -

'Whore. Murderer.'

A shocked silence followed. And then to everyone's surprise the girl began to speak in a clear, well modulated, and pleasing voice.

`Sir.' she began. `I don't know you but you seem to think I make a living by means of prostitution. You should know that I am built without the human organs of reproduction, and so this is physically impossible. And, under my present living arrangements I have no need of money. You also say I am a murderer - you should know that my programme has an overriding instruction never to cause harm to a human being. This can easily be verified. Murder is therefore also an impossibility.'

This quite lengthy speech was heard in silence and was finally greeted by a hum of surprise which the coroner stopped with some difficulty.

Gaining control he then addressed Mary.

`You are known as Mary Lynn?' To which the girl answered `Yes.'

`You understand that we only want you to tell us exactly what happened in the building from the time you entered with the young man until the time you left, on...' - here he gave the date.

In the same clear voice the girl told her story to a silent captivated court.

`Yes,' she said. `I met the boy outside and asked him help me find a power socket, to which he agreed, and took me to a large building. Inside he directed me upstairs where on the second landing was an electrically active power-point. The boy was behind me as I plugged myself in. On connection my system completely closes down so as to conserve power during the charging phase, so I am unaware of anything that happens until charging is complete approximately four hours later when my system is re-activated.

'I was then alone and went down stairs and left the building'

'But you must have passed the body of the boy on the stairs as you left?' The coroner queried.

'I did pass something on the stair but my sensors detected no human life signs.'

By now she had captured the sympathy of nearly everyone in that court room with her pleasing demeanor, and her sheer feminine magnetism.

The exception was Anton's father who was wiping away tears. He arose and directing himself to Mary Lynn, said in a weepy voice, 'My son is dead, have you no feelings, no compassion.'

All eyes were on the girl. William had no idea how she would react.

Then in the same quiet voice Mary Lynn made her second speech of the day.

'I understand that it is customary to say one is sorry for your sad loss, but I am not equipped with human feelings. However you do have such experiences and so I hope that in due course time will lessen them for you.'

After a second or two whilst this was assimilated the court room rang with applause.

No-one had any further questions, and apart from some formalities that was it.

The coroner's report came out soon after and reflected most people's view.

He concluded that Anton's death was an accident - he simply fell down the stairs when under the influence of drugs.

***

Much later, William was relaxing in the sitting room with Mary Lynn in the easy chair opposite. They had been discussing the case.

After a long silence Mary Lynn, in voice so quiet he hardly heard it, uttered the words that froze his blood and haunted his every waking hour for the rest of his days -

`It was either him or me!' She said.

JML
28/12/2006

⟪ **IN A WORD** ⟫

*I*n the infinite variety of English language usage it must be a rare thing for a way of expression to be the cause of a serious and ultimately disastrous influence on someone's marriage. But in this case it was.

Marion and Albert Spink were a matched pair like vest and pants, or fish and chips. In their manner of speech they were radically different yet it was just this which held them together. Each had an unusual manner of speaking which dovetailed with the other to their mutual satisfaction and understanding.

The massive amount of reading that Marion indulged in as a growing girl was the root cause of her way of expression. She had taken in all she could lay her hands on from romantic novels to medical histories and technical journals. Unfortunately her understanding had lagged behind this tremendous intake of words. The sad result of this was an almost completely arbitrary use of language.

But this was not her worst failing - this was that she just never stopped.

So how then were these two matched?

Well, Albert hardly ever spoke, and when he did his own repertoire of words could probably be counted on one's two hands.

Were you to be around when the pair were approaching it sounded much like hearing an oncoming train. One would become aware of a slowly growing almost continuous sound in which no words were distinguishable. This would be interrupted at almost regular intervals by a deeper very short blast of noise. Maximum loudness would be as the couple drew level at which point words might sometimes be distinguishable, whence it gradually drifted into silence as the couple drew away.

'mumble....mumble.....mumble.........' 'YBUT.' 'mumble.....mumble.....' 'YUS.'

'...and her dog snifferised dreadedly,' 'EYE.' '-emolumising all the spherics,'

'OH I.' 'smotherising.' 'CERTN.' '....mumble...... mumble......mumble.....'

They would go.

They understood each other perfectly, it was only when they were in communication with someone else that misunderstandings arose. In these instances life became a struggle.

'Good morning Mrs Spink, How are you?' - A well meaning neighbour.

'I'm sufferising from influentials. The GPO says that I must adjourn to bed but there is a monstrosity of jobs to do, and Spinks shows no inclemencies to do any.

'Oh dear! I'm sorry to hear that. I hope you'll soon be better.'

They had met at a mutual friend's wedding, found that they were compatible and after several misunderstandings got married and set up house together. It was assumed by all their acquaintances that they were reasonably content, but as Albert hardly ever uttered a complete word and Marion was difficult to comprehend, their married bliss or the lack of it was an unknown quantity.

Albert had a local labouring job. He was told by the foreman to shovel this from here to there, and as there was little need for further explanation he collected his wage at the end of the week which with overtime was enough for the pair to live on.

Their only difficulties arose when any discussion or negotiation was required but these were nearly always resolved to Marion's benefit by the other party finally giving in, out of sheer despair.

But this happy situation was doomed.

That winter was mostly cold and very wet, and on successive days poor Albert arrived home from work much the worse for wear. Marion insisted that he stood in the porch until he stopped dripping.

The inevitable happened - Albert contracted a heavy cold.

He was a tough chap, and would normally have ridden out the infection and returned to work in a few days, but this time was different.

The cold went, but he finished up with a very sore throat.

It persisted so they found themselves in the doctor's waiting room - tenth on his list.

They were called in.

Marion sat in the only chair.

Albert stood.

`Well now! What appears to be the problem?' He addressed Marion - a bad start this.

`It's the throttle, the window pipe, I think it's inflamable.' Said Marion.

`I'm sorry,' said the doctor, `I don't understand.'

`The vocalising cordions are stressalised.' Marion explained lucidly.

`Ah, a sore throat?' The doctor thought he had got to the bottom of the problem.

`YUS,' said Albert over Marion's shoulder.

The doctor stood and walked round the desk to Marion, reached down with a spatula in his hand, and said `Open as wide as you can please.'

Marion responded by duly opening her mouth whilst looking considerably puzzled.

The doctor examined her thoroughly and stood back, also looking puzzled.

'Well!,' he said, 'whatever the problem was, it's gone now. You are all clear - in fact I have seldom seen a more healthy throat.'

It dawned on Marion.

'No it isn't me, he's the one whose invalidated.' She pointed at Albert.

Now thought the doctor, we may just be getting somewhere.

Husband and wife swapped places and Albert suffered a very thorough examination at the end of which the doctor addressed Albert with his findings.

'Yes, you do have a slightly inflamed throat. But you also have another problem that you must have been born with.' He paused to let this sink in.

'I imagine that you have always found speech to be somewhat painful?'

Albert nodded.

'You have some extra skin on your larynx, your vocal chords. The good news is that this fault can be rectified with a simple operation. It would of course be on the National Health.'

Albert sat there looking worried for some minutes, then as the meaning of the doctor's pronouncement sank in, a smile began to invade his face, a smile which quickly changed to a grin of delight. They were the best words he had heard in his life.

And so arrangements were made for Albert to have the operation.

It was as the doctor said, a simple procedure, so Albert would be clear to return home after just twenty-four hours.

The great day came, and they arrived at the local hospital on the right day and in good time. They found reception.

Marion as usual decided to be spokesman.

'He's here for his surgeration,' she announced to the neatly dressed receptionist.

'I'm sorry?' she queried.

'He's to have bits eradicated, due to the doctor.' Marion explained.

'Have you got a letter?' The receptionist asked finally latching on to the one word - doctor - that she understood.

Marion produced the letter, and from then on things moved relatively smoothly.

The following day Marion collected a drowsy Albert who was clutching a plastic bag which contained medication and instructions on what not to eat.

Albert was dreadfully disappointed with his operation. He found it even more painful to speak and even gave up completely resorting to using sign language and sitting around looking sorry for himself.

***

But time and the medication were busy working in his favour.

Three long weeks had gone by, when Albert who was seated watching television split some tea from the mug he was holding. The stuff landed on their relatively new carpet where it lay - a brown stain, at Marion's feet.

She paused, then turning angrily to Albert.

'Now just notify what you have perpetrated. I'll never eswage it off.' She said angrily.

Before he could stop himself Albert said -

'Look here, it was an accident, I couldn't help it. I'll go and get a wet cloth and that bottle of carpet cleaner you bought, and you'll see it will come up as good as new.'

It was difficult to decide who was the more astonished by this, the longest speech Albert had ever made in his life. Marion continued to look cross but was so surprised she was silenced the first time in their married life. Albert on the other hand smiled and then started to laugh. He laughed with the pure joy of being able to talk without it being painful.

At first everything was OK. Albert was used to Marion's manner of speech and so conversation between them continued as before but with Albert contributing more of his share.

It was in conversation with others that the problem arose - and grew to disastrous proportions.

Whenever Marion spoke, Albert would translate her utterance into understandable English for the benefit of the listener.

This habit annoyed Marion greatly. But what was worse - Albert began to correct Marion. It got to the point when every time she spoke he would pipe up with his translation followed by an explanation of what she had got wrong and why.

And having found his voice Albert couldn't shut up, he just never stopped talking, and now Marion afraid of being corrected was confined to a stressful silence.

Was that the end for them?

No it wasn't.

They evolved a neat solution.

Marion had bought Albert a silver pen for his birthday and this pen was their salvation.

Whomsoever held the pen was allowed to speak whilst the other was confined to silence - then, and only when ready the pen was handed over for the other to reply.

Did it work? It certainly did, after all they very much loved each other.

JML
28/2/2007

⸙ **THE SOUND OF BRASS** ⸙

Millington prize brass band was recognized by those who followed these musical specialists, and by the results of many competitions, as being one of the finest in the country. Formed in the hey-day of coal mining nearly all the players had been underground workers. Now since the mine was closed they had a variety of jobs from farm hand to council officer, and it was becoming increasingly difficult to keep up to scratch with rehearsals and replacing retiring members. But there they were - still one of the top five.

A key member of Millington's was their number one tuba player. Not only was he the best player they had but he also wrote all their prize winning arrangements. Charlie Endscope had been with the band since its inception and was worshipped by the much younger and more recent recruit the number two tuba -Jimmy Slade.

Charlie recognized Jimmy's eagerness and potential and was grooming him as his own replacement when he eventually ran out of puff. They were good pals and were often at each other's houses sharing vitals with the elder man's wife or Jimmy's widowed mother, or enjoying pints at the Feathers. Both men were popular with the rest of the band and enjoyed the benevolent eye of their conductor and manager Harry `Dog' Smith.

Now as can happen in life, Charlie was so wrapped up in the band, attending every rehearsal, practicing, schooling his protogee, and planning scores for the next competition, not to mention his job as a bus driver, that he completely failed to notice things were sliding down the scale in the home. In a word he was no longer playing any bedtime music.

Nancy, his wife was still reckoned to be a good looking wench, even in Millington locally noted for the attractive qualities of its women. Charlie himself was a good fit bloke, unmarked by his long stint in the mine.

Married when times were better their son had seen the light when the mine shut and moved to the city where he had set up a small but flourishing small parts engineering business, and was now largely out of their daily lives.

Very gradually Charlie's fingering exercises were concentrated more on his tuba when they would have served him better had they been experienced by Nancy. And she, with time to spare, was becomingly increasingly frustrated. It was not that she did not enjoy the band - she did, and supported her man in his musical endeavours - but she required him to play more intimate tunes.

Although he didn't register it, for Harry discord was beginning to sound at home. The current score had run its course and a crescendo was approaching fast. There would be no prize at the end.

Nancy was not getting any younger and had realized that there was more to life than a few notes however well they were strung together.

Now it was unfortunate that just at this moment the Band's number one cornet player Tom Green found himself without a woman. A confirmed bachelor he enjoyed the opposite sex and had quite a few conquests to his name. Handsome, well to do, and carefree he was considered by the ladies to be something of a good catch for the one who could land him, but so far he had managed to escape the net.

As with most of the band Tom was welcome in their homes for a bite or a swift half and a chat.

Trouble was that lately he had taken to visiting Charlie's more often, and when Charlie was not present. And in this he was not discouraged by Nancy who, it has to be said, was somewhat flattered by his attention. It was plain to all but Charlie that Tom was very keen on Charlie's Nancy and was beginning to make no secret of the fact. The only person who seemed not to realise this was Charlie himself.

The situation was potentially explosive.

Young Jimmy tried to alert his mentor with hints which fell on deaf ears.

`Er, Charlie, it's none of my business but don't you think you should keep an eye on Tom and your missus? He fancies her you know.'

`It's OK, Tom's a good mate. Now let's do that passage again from the top, this time though with a bit more emphasis on those last two bars.'

And they did.

And while they were practicing in the village hall Tom was at Charlie's gazing with open admiration at Nancy's comely figure, his mind awash with desire.

***

The run-up to the year's first competition, just two weeks off, was under way - when Tom unable to contain himself any longer suggested to Nancy that they spent a night together at a hotel in the country.

Nancy was flattered and tempted, but she didn't say yes - but neither did she say no.

At heart a good girl, she loved her Charlie, so she decided to give him a chance to recover that which they were in danger of loosing. She knew Charlie would not forgive her straying, especially with Tom and the whole band knowing.

She told Charlie to cancel his next rehearsal - `We must talk,' she said.

Charlie was mystified, it was so out of character for Nancy to be so serious, and fearing she was about to disclose that she had a terminal health problem or something equally horrifying, he agreed.

They sat with the kitchen table between them.

After a long pause with Charlie looking at his wife who was clearly close to tears and him sat wondering what in heaven was about to come.

`OK love, what's up?' He asked eventually.

Nancy jumped and waded all the way in.

`Charlie, you've not made love to me for ages,' she said tearfully, and waited.

Charlie was too stunned to speak. Was this all it was about? Soon fixed, he thought.

`I don't think you love me any more. You love your tuba and the band instead.'

And before Charlie could reply, she added fatefully -

`Tom has asked me to go away with him.'

Charlie sat stunned for a second time, but now his whole world had fallen apart.

Then, mustering all his courage, he said -

'Will you go?'

Nancy started to cry.

'I don't want to, but he seems to love me and you don't,' she managed between sobs.

At this Charlie's whole being reacted.

He leaped up, dashed round the table and took Nancy in his arms. He protested his love for her, saying he would deal with that gigolo Tom.'

He tried to kiss Nancy, but she squirmed away and gazed at him uncertainly.

'I'll see he never blows another note on that cornet of his.'

At this Nancy dried her eyes and took control of the situation she had provoked.

'No Charlie, this is about you and me not about him. If you say or do anything, all the band will know, and we will look foolish and you don't want that. If you want us to stay together you most show me that you really do love me, and I mean by loving me.'

At this Charlie sat down again, and looking miserable, eventually said -

'I'm truly sorry love. Can you give me another chance?'

He knew in his heart that it was his last, next time he would loose her and with her his world.

She did not reply immediately, but then very quietly -

'Oh, of course I will.'

***

Later Charlie phoned Harry to say he couldn't make rehearsal that evening, something he had never done before. He offered no explanation.

At rehearsal, Jimmy did his best to take Charlie's number one tuba part but the band missed Charlie's sure tones.

Tom knew something was amiss and could not concentrate, throwing the cornets into chaos.

The rehearsal was a shambles and Harry was in despair.

***

The following day Charlie was on late shift, but when young Jimmy called for his usual hour of tuition he was told politely - `Not today lad if you don't mind.' He was showing Nancy that he had one or two improvisations up his sleeve, and she was showing him her appreciation.

It all seemed wonderfully new to both of them.

***

At the next rehearsal the band were all present and before they got down to matters serious, Charlie managed a quiet word with Tom.

`Tom, you are welcome in my house but only when I'm there or I will straighten out your cornet for you.'

The whole band knew something was wrong and the result was a complete lack of teamwork and some of the worst playing they had produced.

Rumours circulated putting everyone on edge, and Charlie showed his distrust of Tom. Harry was in despair when out of the blue came an angel.

It was down to young Jimmy.

He was attending night school as a member of their orchestra. Over coffee during the break he had sat with a young and very personable lady who was competent with several instruments including the cornet. Tentatively he asked her if she had considered joining a brass band. To his surprise she jumped at the idea saying that her farther had been a cornet player in the renowned Dobson Brass Band until it disbanded some years previously.

Jimmy knew Harry was looking for another cornet player, and after hearing Jill play Harry immediately took her on.

Tom was bowled over with Jill and the appreciation seemed mutual.

Charlie relaxed and spent more time at home, 'improving his technique' he said.

The upshot was that Millington came second, sadly pipped to first by just one point, but was the highest they had ever been.

'Next year,' said Harry, and was resoundingly cheered.

JML
3/1/2007

GEMSTONE

Fate all too often steps in to alter, for good or for evil, even the best laid of human plans. It strikes without warning sometimes choosing the most unsuspecting moments and in the least likely situations. It is the one thing in life against which there is no possible protection.

Simon Carver's meeting with fate came with a bang.

Out on the local golf-course on his own he was putting in some intensive practice for the forthcoming Captain's Cup match. He was so engrossed that he hardly noticed that the sky had grown overcast and the air heavy.

Fate dictated that he was on the high and very exposed 13th when it happened.

There was an immense flash followed immediately by a dreadful rending of the air and a deafening crash. Where moments ago there was a man teeing up on the green there now was a sorry mound of smoldering clothing, and a horrible smell of charred flesh. Simon Carver would not make the match or any other appointment on this earth.

It was some time before Simon was missed and the ambulance called. He was pronounced dead on arrival and the usual formalities swung into action. It fell to the Captain to break the news to Mrs Carver.

'Please come in,' she invited opening the door with a warm smile of welcome.

'Please do sit down. Would you like a drink?'

Then noticing the Captain's grim expression, 'Is anything wrong?'

'I'm sorry, but I have some terrible news,' he began.

'Don't tell me,' she interrupted. 'Simon has been struck by lightning. How is he?'

'I'm truly sorry, but I'm afraid he's dead. How did you know?'

'News travels fast, we heard someone had been struck, but no-one knew who.'

The Captain waited for her reaction, but none came. Mrs Beth Carver simply poured herself a glass of wine, sat back and looking coolly at him, asked - 'Tell me did he suffer?'

'As far as we know he never knew what hit him, it must have been instantaneous,' he assured her.

'Just where was it?'

'On the 13th .'

'Yes it would be, that was always his bogie.'

The Captain was amazed but grateful for her composure and after the usual sentiments of sympathy he took his leave.

The marriage of Simon and Beth Carver was one in name only. For many years they had led separate lives, he with his business and his golf and her with her cruises and reading circle. And so she got straight down to business - where was his will? She knew he had drafted one but how far had it got - she was desperate to know. She found it in the desk in his study.

And she got a shock.

Simon had amortised everything he could including the house, and having turned it into cash had invested it all on the purchase of just one item -

A solitaire diamond.

What was worse he had bequeathed this jewel to a Miss Gertrude Sellers of whom Beth had never heard.

The will document was clearly the original and was signed by her husband and two witnesses. A quick phone call to the solicitors whose name was on the envelope which had contained the will, ascertained that they did not have the will nor a copy of it but they had assisted Simon in drafting it, and were aware of its content. And no - without the signed and witnessed document this would not stand up in a court of law.

It took Beth but a moment or two to come to her decision, she angrily tore up the will form and burnt it. She felt much better.

She then thoroughly searched the house for the diamond - without success.

***

The death and funeral arrangements were published in the area newspaper, the date of the latter being ten days hence.

It was just one day after publication when Beth answered the door to an extremely attractive and well dressed young woman who announced herself as Miss Sellers, and asked politely if she could speak to Mrs Carver.

Beth's curiosity overcame her antipathy and Gertrude was invited in.

She didn't muck about.

Withdrawing a copy of Simon's will from her bag she waved it at Beth.

'So where is this diamond he promised me?' She demanded.

To her astonishment Beth laughed.

'I'm afraid I have no idea, I've searched everywhere for it,' she said. 'But perhaps you might tell me how you know my late husband?'

'I'm, er - was, his mistress, we met often when he was on his so-called business trips.'

And she made it plain that she did not believe Beth's not knowing where the diamond was. After which she gave Beth her phone number and took her leave saying she would return for it when it did turn up.

The next caller was an untidy pallid individual with a threatening way with him. He introduced himself as Bert and told Beth that Simon owed him some ten thousand pounds in gambling debts and showed her a sheaf of IOU's each with Simon's signature. He added that Simon had shown him a large diamond which he used as security against the debt, and could he now have his money please - at which he looked most unpleasant. He also did not believe Beth. He left his phone number and turning to Beth - put his face up close to hers - said -

'Please don't do anything silly lady. I know about diamonds.' And he was gone.

Then came the manager of the building society which now held the mortgage on the house, and it came as no surprise to Beth that Simon had used the diamond as collateral.

Finally there was the manager of the local branch of one of our larger banking groups. His reason for calling was very different -

He told her that he, or rather the bank, had the diamond in safe keeping.

It was held in a safety deposit box. He had seen it but did not know its value. When the death certificate had been verified he would release it into Beth's ownership. But he added there was the matter of the one hundred thousand pound loan Simon had taken out against the diamond.

Beth thanked him and said she would be in touch.

Now you might be forgiven for thinking - poor Beth - she looks like finishing up broke due to her husband's wayward life-style. But she had independent means which, even if the worst were to happen would allow her a comfortable life in spite of this mess.

Nevertheless it required sorting. So she called all the above involved parties to the house for the day following Simon's funeral.

***

The internment took place without a hitch, and Beth was intrigued to notice that all the claimants were present. Only Gertrude Sellers showed any emotion.

The next day was warm and sunny, so Beth arranged a table and chairs out in the garden with snacks and drinks. This was on the wide lawn at the rear of the house flanked on two sides by flower beds in full bloom and a mass of colour. On the third side, away from the house and separating the lawn from an expanse of open fields was a small fast running stream which added its friendly chuckle to the scene. Birds were everywhere and the air was alive with the buzz of insects.

One by one they arrived and took their place at the table. Beth and Gertrude Sellers were the only ones showing no sign of nervousness.

Bert came with a large dog of indeterminate breed which he tethered to the leg of his chair and told it to sit, which it did.

When they had eaten and partaken of a drink Beth opened the proceedings and in doing so she triggered a chain of events that no-one could have foreseen.

'Right!' She said, turning to the bank manager -

'Let's see what all this is about, will you please show us this wonderful diamond?'

The manager produced a small square of black velvet and laid it carefully on the table where they could all see it. Then opening his brief case he took out a small safety deposit box, produced a key from his pocket and turned it in the lock.

Beth then gave him Simon's ring of keys of which he selected one and turned it in the second lock. He then slid the lid open and using a pair of tweezers and a slightly shaking hand he gently lifted the diamond out and placed it on the black cloth where it sat looking disappointingly ordinary.

Bert swore under his breath.

'Now,' he said, 'that is some diamond.'

'If it's genuine.' he added.

'Check it,' said Beth.

At this fate gave a hollow chuckle, the timing was perfect.

Bert produced an eye-glass and a pair of jeweller's tweezers and carefully lifted the gem from the cloth, and with the glass in place he turned the stone so the sun lit its facets and rays of refracted colour flashed out to dazzle the onlookers.

After what seemed an age Bert declared the stone to be genuine with its appropriate De-Beers number and identification, and he estimated its value as at least half a million pounds sterling.

To which statement there were gasps of appreciation around the table as each considered there was easily enough to go round.

Now! Said fate.

Onto Beth's lawn the next door's black and white cat strode with slow deliberation in the sure knowledge that Beth did not own a dog. It reached the middle of the lawn where it paused and stretched luxuriously in the warm sun.

Things then moved very quickly indeed.

Bert's dog leapt to its feet, and with a loud bark lunged with all its powerful muscular force at the cat, which, not wishing to be a meal for the dog raced away across the lawn, followed by the dog.

The dog's lead tightened, and the leg of Bert's chair to which it was secured was jerked into the air.

Bert's arms flailed as he tried to recover his balance, and the assembled group watched open mouthed as the precious stone made a twinkling arc through the air before it fell with an ever so gentle plop into the stream, where it settled in amongst the tens of thousands of small stones that made up the bed.

Gone.

***

After a fruitless search of the stream, the assembled group, with Bert cursing his unfortunate dog, dispersed to sort out their finances as best they could.

Henceforth Beth would occasionally peer into the stream's clear depths just in case she might find the diamond.

This honour was left to Beth's young nephew, who some years later, was fishing the stream with a net when he brought to show Beth an unusual translucent stone he had found. It was subsequently shown to be of the identical size and cut of the missing diamond -

But it was a clever fake.

JML
7/1/2007

◈ **CHAIN REACTION** ◈

The phrase 'chain reaction' is normally associated with atomic energy in the form of a run-away nuclear power station or an atomic bomb, but in this case the active elements were people, and the effect on their lives was nearly as deadly.

It was dusty work. He had been driving for four hours, the road was straight as far as the eye could see and tiredness was starting to be a worry.

Joe Petty was covering the seemingly endless miles of the Eyre or The Great Western Highway in his hired Holden. He had been sent out to Australia from the UK as an urgent replacement for a sales colleague who 'was taken crook'. So far the trip had been successful. His last stop, Perth, had seen him leave with a nice bunch of sales, and he was justifiably pleased with himself.

There was one good reason why Joe was keen to be back in the UK on time and he was determined not to be delayed.

He only had to make the remaining few hundred miles back to Adelaide where he would swap the car for a plane and then another plane and home, a mere three days.

He had enjoyed the trip but it had taken its toll and he was now anxious to be back.

The car was running well and the ruler straight road required little effort. The big green truck behind him and the red pick-up in front had been with him for the last hundred or so miles and he was relaxed about them, and he wondered if they would still be with him at the end of the trip.

Then suddenly his peace of mind was shattered as the metallic tones of his mobile phone rent the air. A quick glance at it on the passenger seat indicated that the call was from the UK. He realized it must be important as it must be about two a.m. back home.

A pull-off was coming up so feeling that a break would be welcome he left his two fellow travellers and parked, turned off the engine and reached for the phone.

***

Some considerable time earlier, several days in fact, at a small engineering works in north Manchester, Barry Sideley was starting his afternoon's toil and having enjoyed a good lunch and a pint at the local pub was suddenly and violently sick.

Worse was to come and before the day's end his heart would replace his stomach as the centre of his pain.

He seemed to recover a little and a colleague was detailed to take him home. Barry had been married for some twenty years and so far they were without issue. His wife had a part-time job in a local estate agent's office and this was one of her working days.

So it was some surprise to him that not only was her car on the drive but with it was another which he did not recognize.

Having obtained Barry's assurance that he would be OK the colleague drove off leaving a very bemused Barry inserting his key into the front door lock.

You may be excused for guessing what happened next.

There was something of a scuffle in the master bedroom and a half naked bloke he had never seen before emerged carrying a bundle of clothes.

`I'm sorry,' he said, and dashed past Barry, and was down the stairs and driving away quicker than it takes to tell, leaving a sad and potentially violent situation behind him.

Barry took in the scene of his wife half naked standing beside a tumbled bed trying to look contrite and angry at the same time, and he felt sick again.

He turned on his heel and slowly descended to their living room where he poured himself a liberal whisky and sat trying to decide what action to take.

Martha took her time, allowing Barry to arrive at a decision. His action would depend on just what his wife would have to say for herself. If she was sorry he hoped they might sort things out.

To his astonishment she stormed into the room and demanded to know why he had come home at this unusual time without phoning her first.

Barry was horrified, and after a long silence looked directly at his wife and said -

`I was taken ill, and I still feel rotten.' He paused to recover some sanity, then - `I know things have not been great between us for some time, but it would appear that you have found an alternative solution. What you have done I can forgive, but what I cannot accept is your hostile attitude which I am unhappy to say means that at least for the foreseeable future we cannot possibly live together.'

Martha looked even more angry, but before she could speak Barry continued.

`The house is in my name, so you will pack what you need for now and leave. I don't care where you go, but from now on you no longer live here.'

Barry had spoken. Martha knew better than to argue. So she packed some things and left.

Fortunately for Martha her older and unmarried sister Jane was away on holiday with her current amour in Italy, and she had a key to Jane's house.

She let herself in, and phoned Jane with the story of what had just taken place.

Martha and Jane were close, And Jane decided to return home to comfort her sister. Her boy-friend Allun Stebbs judged that this was a purely family matter and he would only be in the way. Besides he was enjoying himself, so he would stay on.

***

Allun was something of a keen mountain walker and so after a day to relax he drove into the hills and armed with a map and guide book set off for a good day's climb in almost perfect weather. His confidence on this occasion was however misplaced.

It was just after lunch that Allun strode confidently to the edge of the path in order to photograph the tremendous view along the valley far below, when a stone he had his foot on, rolled away leaving him waving his arms uselessly about and unbalanced.

In the fall he broke his leg.

Fortunately the path was a busy one and Allun was soon being stretchered down to the local hospital where his leg was promptly set by a doctor who had clearly seen plenty of such cases.

Whilst in hospital he realized that he would need help getting home, after all he couldn't even drive his hired car. So he telephoned his younger and also unmarried brother.

Samuel (Sam) was in one of the inevitable meetings his Company seemed to love to indulge in when his brother's call came. So he took advantage of the situation to leave the meeting to answer it, having explained to the chairman that his brother would not have contacted him at work if it were not important.

His immediate boss was sympathetic and released Sam for as long as it took him to get his brother back home.

Sam then phoned Jane who was up to her ears trying to sort out her wayward sister and asked Sam to keep her posted and to give Allun her sympathy, and to tell him not to be so clumsy in future.

Women!

So Sam packed a light haversack with a few overnight things and managed to obtain a seat on an afternoon flight to Italy for the following day.

Little did he anticipate what high drama he would be involved in before he finally boarded.

***

The day was clear warm and sunny as Sam paid his taxi and strode confidently into the Airport concourse. He was too early to check-in and so he made for the bar.

'May as well treat it as a holiday.' He thought.

As he sat at the bar he scanned the other would-be travellers. He noted the usual business men in suits with their lap-tops and brief cases looking either bored or anxious. Several holiday makers in casual clothes with a variety of small luggage were enjoying pre-flight drinks and smiling and laughing a lot.

The only attractive girl he could see was a dazzling beauty looking far too young to be so heavily pregnant. He thought she seemed to be too nervous to be enjoying herself. By the way she kept glancing at the arrivals monitor she was clearly meeting someone.

Sam knew he was on his way and began to relax.

He could not have been more wrong. Events of high drama would ensure that he missed his arrival in Italy by a whole day.

As happens with these events, there was no warning.

The atmosphere in the bar, cut off as it was from the concourse by glass panels and a swing door, was quiet, even subdued.

Suddenly the peace was shattered by a scruffy youth bursting in shouting angrily at the top of his voice - he was so incoherent as to make it impossible to discern his meaning. This would in itself have been enough to alert the security staff, but that was far from the most frightening thing.

The ranting figure's face was hidden by a black balaclava and in his waving fist he held a gun.

It became a scene of panic and pandemonium.

Some people dived for what cover there was behind tables or chairs. Some sat rigid with fear. The bar staff vanished and an alarm started to wail.

The figure continued to shout uncomprehendingly and wave the pistol. But then things moved very quickly indeed.

The door burst open and two men in uniform entered brandishing automatic rifles.

They shouted at the youth telling him they were armed and to drop the weapon and to lie face down.

The youth tried to turn to confront the two men and there was a terrific bang as he fired his gun at them, and missed.

The men knew their job and didn't waste another moment. There was an ear splitting rattle as a shower of bullets hit the youth who fell and lay still, in a growing pool of his own blood. The two men proceeded to make sure that he was now harmless.

More security men arrived and after removing the body and taking everyone's name and address, cleared the bar.

It was only then that Sam remembered the girl.

It was a while before he discovered her and he got a shock. She was huddled in a corner white with fear and holding her stomach with both hands.

'It's all over now,' he said. 'You can relax.'

At this she started to cry and he thought at first that she had been hit.

'Are you OK?' He asked.

'No,' she replied. 'It's my baby. It's not due for three weeks but I think it's coming now.'

Sam had a moment of panic, but quickly gathered himself together and after telling the lass to stay put, he found the airport nurse who was comforting some of the recent occupants of the bar. He took her to the girl and she quickly took control.

As the girl was loaded into an ambulance she held on to Sam and asked him tearfully not to leave her. And so Sam found himself in the ambulance and on his way to hospital.

On arrival the girl whose name he now knew to be April was taken by stretcher to the delivery ward and Sam was taken along too as the staff assumed him to be the father. On reaching the ward Sam was politely asked to wait in the big waiting room and he was advised that as April might require surgery he would not be allowed to be present at the birth.

By now Sam was exhausted and sat down grateful to be able to relax and decide what he ought to do next. Still concerned for April he asked the staff to find out who he should contact, so they gave him a few minutes with her. He found her mildly sedated and relaxed. She thanked him and pleaded with him to stay, and after a search for her bag gave him her husband's name and mobile phone number. It appeared that he was on his way back from Glasgow by plane after seeing an aged aunt who was unwell, and she gave him the flight number.

Firstly Sam contacted his brother to tell him he would be delayed - explanations later. Next he tried to phone April's husband and discovered that he was still in Glasgow - his flight having been delayed by the shooting. Persistence paid off and he was able to explain the situation to the lad without mentioning how near Alice had been to the action. Pete, the husband said he would be there as soon as possible and to give April all his love.

Sam was just able to reassure April as they wheeled her away to deliver her.

***

It was two a.m. when Sam and the newly arrived, nervous, and anxious Pete heard the first healthy cry of Alice's son.

The staff were now aware of Sam's role, nevertheless at Alice's request he was allowed to join Pete at the bedside of mother and son. She sleepily thanked him and said her son's middle name would be Sam.

It was as Sam was preparing to leave the hospital when he remembered his promise to tell Alice's father the good news. He had learned that dad was somewhere in Australia where the day was well underway. It would be expensive but he decided to try - a promise was a promise after all.

After several false attempts, to his surprise and delight he heard a distinctly English answering voice say -

`Joe Petty here.'

He was through and on a clear connection.

Avoiding any mention of the shooting he told Joe he had a lovely grandson, that Alice had been taken early, that mother and child were doing well, and that her husband Pete was with her.

Joe was so delighted that he failed to ask what Sam's role was in all this.

Much later back in the UK Joe learned just what he had to thank Sam for in helping his daughter. But soon he would have a much, much, more important reason.

***

A very happy Joe replaced the phone, started the Holden, slipped it into first, waited for a good gap in the traffic, eased the car out and up to speed, and settled down to cover as many miles as the day would permit. He hoped to make it to Ceduna where he would stay the night, but this didn't happen.

He had covered just another hundred or so miles when he was stopped by a queue of wagons and cars. A policeman strolled back to him.

'Sorry mate,' he said. 'But there's been a nasty accident up front and it may take a while. Mind if I ask, do you have food and drink?'

Joe assured him that he had provisions, and thanked him, and the policeman walked on to wave the oncoming traffic to a halt.

After about half an hour the police had managed to get the traffic moving slowly in both directions and it was some little time before Joe's car reached the tail end of the accident. Cars and trucks were piled into one another for about a mile. People, police, ambulances and medics were all busy with the injured.

It was as he was passing the very heart of the accident that Joe got the fright of his life - For there, crushed together, into a single mangled heap were the still identifiable remains of the green truck that had been behind him and the red pick-up that had been in front.

The smash had been so bad that no-one could possibly have survived in either vehicle, nor any that might have been in between.

Joe was still shaking when he arrived at the next town and left his car to find a bar for a recovering drink. He was going no farther that day.

***

That night, as Joe lay still dressed on the hotel bed, a good drink by his side, he was enjoying the thoughts of a brand new grandfather; but he was very aware and would never forget that the phone call had saved his life.

`By God, thank you Sam.' He said out loud, and meant it.

JML
11/1/2007

THE UNDERSTANDING

Just about everything in the Tassit marriage was hunky-dory, and had been for some considerable time. Their stable life-style seemed to be the envy of their many friends and acquaintances. Their existence had settled into a well regulated routine in which there was no room for life's usual inharmonious disturbances.

Their ever loving children were married and leading equally stable lives, one in the far north, the other way down south. They visited regularly by arrangement and when they did the normal routine was suspended for the duration. Their son and daughter and their offspring were much loved and their visits were always anticipated with pleasure. Throughout these times the children were given priority and they became the centre of all activities. But the second they left the Tassit household dropped seamlessly back into its regular formula.

Now Arnold and Olive would each claim, if challenged, to be happily married to each other, and in one sense they were. But each had another life. Underneath this placid surface ticked another world altogether different, and potentially explosive.

Olive had a secret lover and Arnold had his clandestine mistress.

In spite of this, neither party gave any hint of these alternative arrangements to the other. It was never ever mentioned, not even alluded to or hinted at. It just did not exist.

You see they each had what they thought of as 'an understanding', you might say it was a Tassit understanding; and even this was never openly alluded to. In spite of its ephemeral nature this understanding was the only glue which held their marriage together.

But its stability was an illusion, mere wishful thinking.

A fragile thing.

Neither husband or wife were good looking, having let themselves succumb to the effects of growing older, and had some time ago ceased to find each other attractive.

In bed on their honeymoon some considerable number of years ago, they had soon discovered they were incompatible, and they only succeeded in procreating by dint of persevering - a procedure they found distasteful and had long ago foregone.

But they seemed content. Arnold Tassit held down a well paid job with a local distribution company, which incidentally meant unusual working hours. And Olive Tassit worked as household manager on the big estate, also well paid and with variable hours. Both man and wife were mentally congratulating themselves on the success of this arrangement when onto this calm surface, one day, a small wavelet appeared. It was easily dealt with but it was the sign of an oncoming storm.

Olive had fallen for a visitor to the estate. Lionel Easy was an easy going, placid kind of chap. Used to the attention of the opposite sex who relished his good looks, he found them too pushy and mostly preferred his own company. Tall, bronzed, ruggedly handsome in a darkish sort of way, he had managed to steer clear of awkward associations. That is until Olive decided to make him her half of the understanding.

She explained the unspoken rules to Lionel to set his mind at rest and assure him that there would be no irate husband chasing him. This appealed to Lionel who dropped his other female hangers-on in favour of Olive.

Now, Lionel also had an understanding.

His wife was an invalid, quite capable of looking after herself but unable to take any part in sexual activities. She had long ago accepted that her husband would satisfy these needs elsewhere, and just as long as he stayed and took care of her, and declared her to be his true love, she was content. Sheila was an unusual woman, and Lionel thought himself a lucky man.

However these understandings were not Olive's main attraction for him.

In spite of his obviously masculine good looks Lionel was the least demonstrative of lovers, and Olive's lack of real enthousiasm for the act was just ideal. The pair of them enjoyed the clandestine aspect of their relationship without needing to satisfy any basic biological necessity. In this they were well suited and content and asked for nothing more.

But a storm was now definitely brewing of which they were completely oblivious.

Arnold's mistress was an altogether different kettle of fish, and it was she who became the eye if the storm, she was it's trigger and its force.

It should have been obvious to Arnold that he had taken on something of a tornado but besotted as he was he didn't see it coming in spite of the obvious signs.

So what was the problem?

For a start Arnold's lady was young, attractive, but above all she was unmarried.

Blonde, tallish, with a real woman's well rounded figure she was a stunner and knew it.

Bernadette was also ambitious. She could have taken her choice of several eligible young studs who tried their best to land her. But she wanted an established older man, a man of some experience.

She chose Arnold. She flashed those deep blue eyes at him and let him know as she displayed that gorgeous body that it could all be his just for the taking.

Bernadette became Arnold's part of the understanding.

Arnold found himself in another world when alone with Bernadette. Highly sexed, she introduced him to every aspect of erotic enjoyment, and he knew for the first time the true meaning of pleasures of the flesh, and he soon became the driving force of their intimacy, much to Bernadette's satisfaction.

These unspoken arrangements lasted for a couple of years.

But Arnold's part was inherently unstable.

Bernadette's girl acquaintances were getting married and settling down. They wanted to meet `her man' but this was not possible. They tended to gang together and talk about babies and house furnishings - leaving her out.

And she was getting older.

So she began to ask Arnold to divorce his wife and marry her. It soon became her main topic of conversation, that is when they weren't making love.

Arnold refused to listen.

So, Bernadette hatched an unholy plan.

If Arnold wouldn't divorce Olive, she - Bernadette, would split them up.

She phoned Olive and without preamble told her that she was a friend of Arnold's and she had something of vital importance to discuss with her, but she wouldn't say what.

Olive knew that she should refuse but female curiosity got the better of her, as Bernadette guessed it would.

They arranged to meet at an hotel out of town. Olive would recognise Bernadette by the orchid she would be wearing.

The day of the meeting arrived, and Olive was there early and made straight for the bar and ordered herself a large gin and tonic which she took to a corner table from which she could see everyone who came and went. For the thousandth time she wondered what this was all about, and for the thousandth time almost changed her mind and left. However, she was not kept waiting long.

When Bernadette entered most of the men present turned to stare, or rather gape. She was just about the most alluring creature most of them had ever seen, and all eyes followed her as she made her way to the bar, where the barman rushed to attend her.

With her cocktail in hand she coolly scanned the room and immediately spotted Olive, who was beginning to wish she was more elegantly dressed. The contrast between the two women was obvious, and Olive felt much the inferior, as of course Bernadette had intended.

Tripping over to Olive's table she held out her hand.

'Hi,' she said. 'I'm Bernadette, and you must be Olive, Arnold's wife.'

It was a statement not a question - a way of showing who was in charge.

'Yes.' Replied Olive.

Bernadette sat down, and looked around. 'Nice place.' She said.

There was a long pause whilst the two women weighed each other up. What they saw filled Bernadette with confidence and Olive with apprehension, and she began to guess what this was all about.

Olive broke the silence. 'Well you wanted to see me?' She said.

Bernadette decided to attack.

'I want you to divorce Arnold so that we can get married.'

This shook Olive.

She had to know.

'Well does Arnold agree?' She asked.

Bernadette avoided the question, much to Olive's relief, and her hopes rose.

'I can offer him so much more than you, and he deserves me.'

'Exactly what can you offer him?' Olive asked, curiosity taking over.

At this point Bernadette played her trump card as she had planned. Leaning across the table she began to speak intimately to Olive all the time closely observing her reactions.

She started by saying how frequently they made love, and what demands Arnold made of her.

She went on to describe what she wore to tantalise him.

- The slow undressing.
- What he did to excite her.
- What he did with his hands.
- What he did with his tongue.

All the time she noted that her words were affecting Olive, who was having great difficulty hiding her feelings.

She then told Olive what she did to Arnold, stressing his enjoyment.

And made it clear that he couldn't get enough.

Olive wanted more - so Bernadette obliged.

But Bernadette had totally misjudged Olive's reaction.

As Olive listened, at first she was jealous, and then intrigued, but soon she began to feel thrills of excitement running through her. She began to understand for the first time what she was missing. There was nothing of this in her dealings with Lionel. And she was amazed at what her husband was capable of - if he could satisfy this eager young woman he must be some lover.

Bernadette paused, and was mentally congratulating herself on the success of her plan, when she was shocked by Olive suddenly standing up and preparing to leave.

Olive leaned across to Bernadette and said -

'I'm sorry, I'll not divorce my Arnold.' She stressed the `my'. Then after a pause -`But I'd like to thank you - you have proved to be most helpful.'

Bernadette simply stared with her mouth open. She had no idea what had gone wrong. All she could do was to watch Olive leave with a new bounce in her step.

***

After some thought, Olive decide to try out her new knowledge on the easy-going Lionel. She made every effort to look enticing with new and very sexy lingerie. As soon as they were alone she sat on his knee and tried to kiss him as Bernadette had so assiduously described.

But this was enough for the very reticent Lionel, and disentangling herself from her embrace, and without a further word he left.

Olive was bitterly disappointed, but she knew Lionel well and was half prepared for a bad reception. The try-out was nevertheless a failure.

The question was - would it work on her husband or was it only Bernadette that could turn him on?

She decided to give it everything.

Firstly she had to get him away from temptation. So she suggested a holiday abroad, to which Arnold agreed and they chose a very expensive hotel on Lake Garda in Italy. In the meantime Olive concentrated on herself. She lost some weight, had a new and younger hair-do, went to a class on make-up, and purchased some new and elegant outfits. She tried them all on and not only was she pleased with the result, but started to feel very sexy indeed.

She cold bloodedly decided that if Arnold did not come up with the goods she would find a man who would. On no account was she going to go through the rest of her life missing out on what Bernadette had shown her.

Now Arnold had noticed the change in Olive and mistakenly thought she might be doing this for her undisclosed lover. But he was delighted with the change and for the first time had real feelings of jealousy.

He thought that given the opportunity he would show Olive what love making was all about.

The holiday came.

The hotel was perfect, their room delightful, and the scenery breathtaking.

After a wonderful meal with good Italian wine they retired early at Olive's suggestion. Once in their room, she asked Arnold to undress her, and he did so, gasping in amazement and delight when he saw her flimsy and very erotic underwear. He had not seen her naked for years and was thrilled by what he now saw. This was a woman he had never known, and she excited him, and he couldn't keep his hands off her.

She even taught Arnold a thing or two, and to her eternal delight she experienced a woman's satisfaction for the first time.

Later they made love again - and again in the early dawn light on the balcony. It was a holiday niether of them would ever forget. They remembered and shared every detail.

***

Back home they knew without discussion that they had a new understanding, one which would last them for the rest of their married life. And Olive never forgot that it was thanks to Bernadette, but of course she never said anything of this to Arnold.

***

Bernadette was shocked when she told Arnold that she had found someone else. Instead of pleading with her, he merely shrugged his shoulders and wished her well.

JML
20/1/2007

⊰ **FAITH** ⊱

*I*n spite of knowing its reputation for bringing misfortune to its owner, he had to have it. After all Angle Halburg had been after it for the last twelve years ever since he was told about it by an Egyptian antiquarian.

The last owner had committed suicide claiming in a letter to his next of kin that the thing had destroyed his life. His family wanted to have nothing to do with it and had put it in the hands of Withins, auctioneers.

You might think that the source of all this fear would be some ugly, perhaps even vicious looking thing, but it was in fact extremely beautiful. Cast in gold, and standing just about four inches high and six inches long, it was a statuette of a female nude. Her figure was perfection. She reclined seductively whilst in one hand she held a scroll, with the other she pointed as if at the viewer. On its base were as yet un-deciphered hieroglyphics. The overall effect was dynamic and mysterious.

Seeing this impressive object was to remember it for ever, it was as if the lady were alive and about to divulge some well hidden secret.

But the thing was also worth a great deal of money, in fact Withins had given it an estimated value of just over one million pounds. They were hoping for a number of would be purchasers who were prepared to ignore the statuette's foul reputation.

Thought to be early Egyptian in origin it was however not cast in that style being more European in its blatant sexuality.

At some point in her long life she had been given the name 'Opal', from the marks on her base.

Angle had looked into the object's history and had concluded that its evil acts were only wrought on those owners who considered its powers to be real. Without such a superstition he believed that it would be powerless. With this clear in his mind he was determined to own it at whatever cost.

That was as his mind saw it - but what was buried in his soul?

The Halberg household was fabulously rich having made a fortune in the second world war manufacturing armaments which they ruthlessly sold to the highest bidder regardless as to which side they were on.

Two younger brothers Tremp and Chas shared the business with Angle. He himself had two sons by his wife Emily, both of which were also in the Halberg company.

It seems that that even in peacetime countries still needed armaments, and the firm continued to do well.

In spite of trying to keep his ambition to purchase Opal secret, the family got to know, and to Angle's worry a family conference was called.

Two days before the auction Angle, his wife and two brothers sat round the big dining table. Tension was in the air and drinks were served to ease matters. Conversation was on other business issues to begin with, but they were people used to direct dealings.

'So that settles the Japanese problem,' said Angle eventually. 'Is that it?'

The rest looked at each other wondering who would start. Eventually Chas began -

'It's about this Opal thing,' he said.

'What about it?' Angle asked.

'We would like to know if you still intend to make an offer for it?'

'And if I do, would you object?'

'I think I am speaking for all of us when I say we think you are crazy, it will bring disaster to us all, just as it has done to others. We want no part of it.'

'So what do you propose to do if I go ahead then?' Angle asked getting angry. He failed to see what it had to do with anyone else.

'Then to protect ourselves we would be forced to disown you.'

Angle was shocked. This he had not expected.

It was as if Opal's influence was starting even before he possessed her.

'You can't be serious.' He was now furious and trying to hide his fear. The continued prosperity of the business depended on their sticking together.

For the first time and close to tears Emily spoke -

'Please don't do this, we do not want to risk the bad luck this thing will bring. I really can't understand why you want it so badly. You don't need it, so why?'

Angle tried to be calm. Lose his temper and he would lose his family.

'Ever since I first heard about Opal it has intrigued me. I am fascinated by the tales of its power over its owner's fate. I have studied all the recorded cases and I believe that it can only wield its powers if the owner believes it can. It will be impotent against a disbeliever. And as I am a convinced disbeliever I will be immune. I have complete faith in Opal's inability to bring me harm.' He paused to let this sink in.

'Besides,' he went on, 'it is a very beautiful work of art and very ancient. And I want it very badly.'

There was a long silence.

Then with his voice shaking with emotion Chas spoke.

'I think that we will not deter you from bidding for this thing, therefore I have the following suggestion. Should you succeed you will keep the item away from our families and our homes, we never want to see it and especially deny any semblance of ownership which will be exclusively yours. Should we come to believe that it is having a bad effect on the rest of the family you will be asked to get rid of the thing or to leave and we will disown you. Personally I hope someone else outbids you for it.'

There was a murmur of approval from the rest of the family.

A chastened and sad Angle said 'OK, but I assure you all you have nothing whatsoever to worry about.'

They didn't - but he did.

***

The day of the auction came and Opal was on display in pride of place as the most expensive item that day. With their possible liability in mind Withins had prepared a brief

GEMSTONE and other fateful tales

history listing all the claimed instances of adverse influence on its various owners.

The gist of this was as follows:-

"The first recorded case was in Gaul some hundred or so years ad. The owner at that time was an unnamed Roman general. How he obtained 'Opal' is not known. He fought bravely but was routed not by the enemy but by bad weather - it snowed in Gaul in mid summer and his troops went down like flies with an affliction we now know as influenza. The man himself fell from his chariot and was trampled by the following horses and died a slow and painful death on foreign soil.

The artifact was then missing for some unspecified period but turned up eventually with some items believed to have been pillaged from the estate of Baron Le-forge during the French revolution. The state claimed ownership and it was displayed in a small museum thought to have stood in the Montmartre district of Paris. The museum was destroyed by fire and the object vanished yet again.

Since then it is known to have had several legal and illegal owners all of whom wish to remain anonymous, but all of whom are recorded as having relinquished it because of the many and various disasters which befell.

It has been blamed for illness, financial ruin, accidents, and even madness and death.

The family of the present owner blame the statuette for his troubles and eventual suicide and are keen to be rid of it.

The result of our assay is :-

The item (lot 133) is cast in solid 22 Carat gold, that is just over ninety per cent pure, the associate metal being high grade silver.

Signed: PPJ
For Withins Auctioneers"

They wanted no comebacks, and had in fact been somewhat reluctant to even handle the item.

But keen interest was evinced by the fact that the auction room was packed. Some late comers even had to stand at the back.

Lot 133 came up eventually, and at first there was a reluctance to begin, but bidding began at the crazily low figure of one thousand pounds. After a tussel at nine hundred thousand, it was finally knocked down to Angle for one million pounds exactly.

So for better or worse it was his.

***

Angle had prepared for this moment and having settled his account with Withins placed a large padlocked crate in the security van waiting outside, which set off immediately. Half an hour later Angle left Withins carrying a plastic TESCO bag in which was Opal and which he popped casually in the boot of his car.

These precautions were justified as the security van was hi-jacked, the guards just escaping with their lives. Doubters blamed the statuette for this misfortune and members of Withins breathed sighs of relief that the thing was no longer on their premises.

In a back street of a local suburb, a 'one up and one down' premises had been purchased and modified by Angle. He had converted the ground floor into a drive-in garage and the upper space into a display room dedicated to Opal . Special lighting, security and protection against fire were all built in.

No one else knew of this place, and Angle went there often.

Well then how did he fare?

His faith in Opal having no effect on his well being was well founded and absolute. After all, he argued, the thing was merely an inanimate object - just a simple lump of metal. He was firmly of the belief that the misfortunes of others was of their own making, or just simply very ordinary bad luck. He was determined that any and all set-backs he may have would on no account be blamed on Opal.

And so it was - at first.

Arriving one day at the secret place, and keen to get in he dropped the keys to the door and they bounced once before vanishing down a waiting grid. - Clumsiness coupled with anxiety he decided.

The staff in his part of the business went on strike for safer premises, part of the roof had collapsed in a heavy storm. - Act of God he concluded.

The Income Tax Authority discovered he owed them half a million pounds and he only just escaped going to prison. - A simple accounting error he argued and wrongfully replaced his loyal accountant.

He was breathalysed after a successful meeting with clients and lost his license. -

He blamed himself and took taxis to see Opal.

Then he had a bad dose of flu which left him somewhat depressed, and in this weakened state he felt the first tiny murmur of doubt.

Of course the family seized every opportunity to say `I told you so.' Particularly as nothing untoward happened to them. Angle was forced to recognise the contrast. It seemed that it was always him or his part of the business that was suffering.

After he was hit by a speeding hit and run motorcyclist whilst crossing the road and had to spend some time in hospital real doubts began to surface. He had too much time to think and began to wonder if there was anything in the evil side of this beautiful, magnificent, treasured object of his adulation.

Fatal. His faith was showing signs of weakening.

Angle could no longer help himself. He tried not to, but every time something went awry he questioned it, and did his best to put it down to simple bad luck.

But it seemed always to seek him out.

As the incidents piled up worry began to affect his health.

At the next family conference for his own sake, they took him to task.

`How much longer are you going to let this go on?' Asked Chas with concern written on his face. `You should get rid of that thing ASAP, before it really does for you.'

Angle knew they were concerned for him.

`That thing, as you call it, happens to be most precious to me,' he said.

But his voice lacked the conviction it once had. The growing list of misfortunes was eating away at his faith in his immunity.

He recovered and for a while began to feel safe.

Sadly his renewed optimism was misplaced. He discovered a lump where one should not be. The specialist told him with a grim face that he had an inoperable cancer. Angle survived a further six months and died a disillusioned and bitter man----- on the anniversary of his purchase of Opal.

The family were certain that the statuette was the cause of his untimely demise at the age of fifty eight.

They debated how to be rid of the thing, and were in for a shock.

Angle's will was read, and he had requested that Opal be taken from hiding and placed in his coffin and buried with him in the family grave. In this way he hoped that its evil would stay with him and not affect anyone else ever again. The keys and directions to Opal's whereabouts were included with the will.

`I don't like it.' Was Chas's verdict.

`Neither do we,' agreed Tremp, `but it is his will, and perhaps the bad will be buried with him.'

And so it was. The precious object was collected from Angle's specially modified house by the two brothers and the solicitor. It was then carefully wrapped so as to be hidden from the funeral directors who were told it was merely some personal items of no value and placed in the coffin which was then sealed in their presence.

Angle was then interred with due ceremony in the family grave in their own grounds.

The atmosphere at the reception was almost gay, with the family's relief that the troublesome thing was now out of sight and out of mind colouring their sadness for the loss of a loved one.

All was OK - for a time.

***

One day, some months later, Chas, now the eldest, had some time on his hands, and was thinking about Angle and his infatuation with Opal. Suddenly he realised that in spite of the thing being buried with his dead brother, ownership of it had in fact legally passed to Emily as Angle's next of kin.

With this realisation came a feeling of heavy dread.

He decided that the only way to be at peace was to get rid of the thing once and for all. So he called a meeting.

'We must do this regardless of Angle's wishes,' he said after explaining his worries.

'Agreed,' answered Tremp,'and it would be nice to recover its value.'

So they made a plan to relieve themselves of the burden of Opal before it could do any more to hurt them and they decided on secrecy.

Under the cloak of darkness they opened the grave, lifted the coffin lid and removed the wrapped object. After replacing the grave material, they stood solemnly as Chas said a few words.

'We are truly sorry dear brother to have disturbed your rest and to have taken that which you desired, but we believe that for the living it will be for the best. May you continue to be at peace.'

'Amen.'

The following day Chas and his brother checked that the seals on the wrapping were still intact and took the object to a qualified assayist whom they paid well to keep his findings secret.

It was then they got a shock. Opal had one more trick in store for them.

They watched carefully as the grey looking professional carefully broke the seals and unwrapped the object. Its gold shone in the light of the angle-poise bench lamp, and they admired its sheer beauty as a work of art once again.

The man weighed the thing in his hand before picking up a scalpel. He looked puzzled as he turned Opal over and scraped at her underside. Screwing an eye lens into place he looked carefully at the scratches, and then at the brothers.

`I take it that you want some estimate as to its worth?' He asked.

The brothers nodded.

`I'd say about fifty quid - at most.'

He looked from one to the other in the silence which followed.

`It's a clever copy, made of lead with a thin coating of gold plating. Here you can see for yourselves.' He thrust the object at them with a magnifying glass.

But there was no need to check, it was obvious where he had scratched clearly showed the lead beneath the gold.

***

Unhappy as they were about the loss of the value of Opal, they were relieved to be free of its supposed influence.

They could put all future misfortunes down to pure bad luck.

How it was removed, by whom, and where it went was never discovered. Had Angle worshipped the fake Opal all this time?

Presumably, if it still exists, somewhere in the world it is reeking its havoc on someone. Should you come across it my strong advice is to banish temptation and have nothing whatsoever to do with it.

The fake was sold to a local dealer for just forty pounds.

JML
27/1/2007

⋖ **THE WARNING** ⋗

*C*an the living receive messages from the dead? For me I have always firmly believed this to be impossible. I feel that all sensory perception ceases on death. But one strange and bewildering instance gave my certainty a good knock.

I was twenty-five and still single when my parents died in a hit-and-run car accident. They were both practical people and had made wills in which they left everything to me. My father had been a successful business man and besides the fully paid for house in which we lived there was a fair sized bank account. I would still need to work but I could afford some luxuries like good holidays and a decent car.

My job as a sales rep for an up and coming office equipment provider not only took me all over the British Isles but also gave me flexible hours and plenty of free time.

Although still single I had a permanent girl friend Susan. Susan Edge lived some fifty mile away and we were both intent on being much closer. We hoped that this relationship would soon be consolidated by marriage, given that we would be able to see much more of each other. To this end I decided to move nearer to my intended and obtained appropriate leaflets from all the local estate agents.

Susan and I then spent a great deal of time and effort looking for a place that I could manage on my own and would be suitable for us both when we got hitched.

We settled eventually on an old-ish detached house complete with all the usual facilities, the inside having been recently thoroughly modernised, and it had a decent sized well kept garden. With three large bedrooms it was amply big enough for us. So I did the necessary and moved in.

I liked it immediately, the place had a cheerful but cosy feel about it, and I soon made it my, soon to be - our, own.

Life was made easier when a chap in his fifties turned up and announced himself as Simon the two days per week gardener employed by the previous owner. His rate was reasonable so we shook hands on his continuing.

Now Simon had to have somewhere to keep his tools, shelter from the rain and to make himself a brew. When I asked him about this he pointed out that the old lean-to tool-shed which he used before would be just fine. This toolshed I had mentally registered and but for a casual glance had never been inside.

So one dull day with little better to do, I gave full reign to my curiosity, picked up the key from its hook in the kitchen (the gardener had the other one), and let myself in.

What I saw was a complete surprise.

There was of course all the appropriate machine tools for maintaining a garden - a lawn-mower, a hedge-trimmer, a chain-saw; and the usual hand tools - spade, fork, rake, edge cutter and so on. A large bench under the only window held smaller tools and a large workman-like vice.

But what attracted my curiosity was on the shelves mounted on the remaining two walls. One had gardening things - pots, seed boxes, rose fertiliser, and the like. But the other had a curious array of stuffed small animals, bones, coloured stones, a jar of feathers for example, and three or four cardboard boxes none of which, judging by the dust had been touched for a long time.

Just then I heard the muffled ring of the house phone and left further exploration for another day.

At the next opportunity I asked Simon what was in the boxes.

'Actually, I have no idea. All that stuff was there when I came.' Was his reply.

'Where you not curious?' I pressed him.

'Yes I often wondered but then they weren't mine so I left them well alone.'

'OK,' I said. 'I'll have a look sometime. They must have been there for a good while judging by their condition, so they can't be important.'

I don't like mysteries, so I determined to find out what the curious boxes contained - and when I did I got an unpleasant surprise.

Blowing the dust of the first two smaller boxes I found that the lid was simply folded down. Inside both was a collection of small bones which for some reason looked surprisingly human. The next box and the largest was stuffed with some old and dry straw. Removing the top layer of this revealed what was clearly the top of a skull.

Nervous now I stopped to consider matters - then believing that the object belonged to some animal I plunged both hands into the straw and gingerly lifted the thing out. As the last bits of straw fell away I nearly dropped what was unmistakably a human skull.

A human skull?

What the hell was it doing here?

I had only questions and no answers.

Eventually I decided to replace the skull in its box and to discuss what to do next with Simon and Susan.

It was several days later that we three sat relaxing in the kitchen each with a large mug of tea, when I decided to broach the subject of the boxes in the tool shed.

'You cannot possibly guess what I found in one of the boxes in the tool-shed,' I began.

'No, we give in.' Susan replied. 'You'll have to tell us.' And she grinned at Simon.

'I'm afraid it's far from funny,'

'Well, go on then we're all agog.'

She grinned at Simon, still thinking I was joking. But Simon looked serious.

I took a deep breath.

'A human skull.'

There was a pause of astonishment, then they both laughed. They were now sure that it was a leg pull.

When I didn't smile they both sat looking at me with disbelief.

'I don't believe you,' Susan said eventually, 'you'll have to show us.'

Simon looked most unhappy.

In the tool-shed I lifted the largest box down and set it on the bench.

'Go on then - would either of you like to open it?' I asked.

They both declined, and stood watching me nervously.

I slowly lifted the lid out of the way, and gingerly took the skull from its resting place and set it down on the bench where it sat looking at us from its blank eye sockets.

It appeared to be grinning.

Susan gasped, and Simon muttered a quiet `Bloody hell!'

After three or four minutes during which no one spoke Susan reacted -

`Please put the damn thing back, I really don't like it. Anyway what's it doing in our shed?'

I returned the skull to its box and we retired to the kitchen to discuss matters.

The atmosphere was distinctly un-funny as three very chastened people sat down and tried to decide what to do next.

Firstly we rejected involving the police for fear of making fools of ourselves, after all there may be a rational explanation for the skulls presence. Next we agreed to contact the previous owner. Finally Susan suggested calling in her cousin, who was an amateur archaeologist, for an educated opinion.

We had problems locating the previous owner and in the meantime Susan's cousin kindly called after being persuaded we weren't pulling his leg. On being presented with the box he removed the skull handling it with professional detachment.

`You were correct not to call the police,' he said, `you see these numbers etched on the base, they are a museum reference number. This item at some time in its life (forgive the irony) belonged to a museum, which one I'm afraid it is impossible to know. Perhaps the person who left it here may be able to advise you. However perhaps I can tell you a little bit more. I think that it belonged to a male person aged at least sixty or so, and he was a native African. These grooves in the bone would indicate that he was probably some kind of witch-doctor or fortune teller. But how he died I have no idea, nor do I know how his skull came to be here. But you can rest easy that it's not a police matter.'

After these comforting words and our thanks the cousin left. Susan and I settled back into our normal routine, and I booked a holiday for us both in Turkey, a country to which neither of us had been.

It was just a week before we left that we received a phone call from the previous owner, a Mr Handon.

Mr Handon told us that the skull was very old and he had forgotten all about it in the anxiety of moving. He told us he was going abroad and would contact us on his return and arrange to come over and tell us all about it. He expressed himself as sorry for any upset it might have caused, and promised to remove the item.

Two days before we left and I was in the tool-shed looking for a length of string when it happened.

It frightened me half to death.

Thinking of it even now, several years later, makes my blood turn to ice in my veins.

I was looking vaguely round the shed for where Simon kept his string.

The skull for some reason was not in its box but was sitting on its shelf facing directly at me, which in itself was odd. It was unnaturally quiet.

Suddenly a voice seemed to come from the skull.

In a low, dusty, whisper it said -

'Do not go. There lies Death.'

There was nothing more, that was all. The words had been clear and there was no mistaking them.

Whipping round to look at the skull I thought I saw a red glow dying away in its blank eye sockets, and I was certain that I had heard the damn thing speak.

I called myself all kinds of idiot, rammed the thing back in its box, and vowed to tell no one - especially Susan.

To say that the incident worried me was an understatement. As we were soon to be leaving for Turkey you may appreciate my concern.

I was utterly convinced that the message was real and was a warning. I tried, in a round about way to persuade Susan to postpone our projected trip, but as my reasons were pretty feeble and I was causing her some anxiety, I desisted. But I did arouse her suspicions that all was not well, which she eventually put down to my doubts about our spending a whole two weeks together and she sought to reassure me that it was going to be just great.

The nearer the leaving date got the worse was my fear. For fear it now was.

As our flight took off I felt a surge of fatalism. I half convinced myself that it had never happened, it was simply my imagination working overtime.

Nevertheless I decided to take every possible precaution to ensure our safety. In this I must confess to making myself into something of a bore.

The plane landed safely. I checked the airport for any gangsters but saw only tourists. I had a word with the coach driver to make sure he had not been drinking. The drive was enjoyable even if I sat on the edge of my seat ready for anything. I double checked our room which was delightful. I had no idea what I was looking for.

Susan was by now showing signs of irritation at my curious antics, so I resigned myself to our fate, which was hard because I really did not wish to be dead. I had in fact come to the obvious conclusion that I probably couldn't change events anyway.

So I did my best to stuff my worry to the back of my mind, and because Susan was Susan we really did have a good time.

Our week in Istanbul was fascinating and I almost forgot about that bloody skull, but later lazing on the sea shore in the second week I had time to think and thus to worry.

I concluded that I would not be altogether happy until we were safely back home.

The sense of relief which came as we disembarked from the taxi outside our house was so strong that it threatened to overwhelm me. The first thing I did was to pour myself a very large drink. The second was to give Susan a kiss to end all kisses. The third was to make myself a promise to be rid of the skull as soon as possible.

Susan was puzzled by my sudden light heartedness, and put it down to my being happy to be back - which in a very real way it was.

I have never, before or since, felt such an overwhelming relief.

***

A couple of days later I tried to contact Mr Handon, and was told by the answering machine that he was not available. I left a message but my call was not returned.

After a week of the same response to my calls I decided to pay him a visit.

Fortunately there was only one Handon in our local telephone book which listed the street and the house number.

It was still quite early in the morning when I knocked on the Handon's door. It opened eventually to reveal a lady I judged to be in her eighties and dressed all in black. It was obvious that she had recently been crying. I explained who I was and she invited me in. She led the way to a comfortably furnished living room and asked me to be seated, whilst she took the easy chair opposite.

I marshalled my thoughts, but before I could say anything Mrs Handon held out her hand for me to shake and began to speak.

'I am sorry not to have replied to your telephone messages but things have been very difficult of late.' Here she paused and dabbed her eyes with her handkerchief.

'My husband left for Africa ten days ago, in response to a call for help from an old and valued friend. I had word that he had arrived then nothing. I tried my best to contact him but to no avail. Then out of the blue I had a call from the Foreign Office to tell me that my husband was flying home and I should go to Brize Norton airfield where he would be landing and they stated the day and the time.' She paused to recover her composure.

'As you may guess this was a surprise, but Mr Handon was like that - I learned early in our marriage to expect almost anything, but this seemed beyond even his limits.

I arrived at the airfield in good time and was promptly and courteously escorted out onto the tarmac just as one of those big RAF transport planes was landing. The thing rolled to a halt and they opened those big doors and wheeled out a coffin.'

Here she broke down and wept openly for some minutes.

'You see,' she went on with some bitterness, 'what no-one had thought to tell me was that my lovely husband had been accidentally shot in a riot in Africa and this was him in the coffin.'

I mumbled words of sympathy and waited - she had not yet finished.

'So you see I've been a bit busy what with funeral arrangements and so on.' She halted - then -

'By the way, I'm sorry, I neglected to ask you what you came about. What was it?'

This was clearly no time to raise topic of the skull, so I told her that it was not important and would do just as well another time.

Mrs Handon then suggested a cup of tea and bustled off to prepare it.

I had time to think whilst she was away and I decided that the damn skull was becoming a nuisance and I would talk the local vicar into giving it a Christian burial in the church grounds.

We were quietly sipping our tea when Mrs Handon said something that completely took my breath away and left me staring at her with open mouth and my tea dribbling down my shirt front.

'Do you know,' she said, 'two days before he was due to leave and we were both sitting in our kitchen, when it went very quiet and we both heard a strange voice. I don't remember the words exactly but it said "not to go", and something about death.

Was it a warning, you think?'

I was too stunned to give a sensible reply, and fell back on words of sympathy.

***

On my way home I realised that the Handons were hearing their strange voice at exactly the same moment in time that I thought I heard the skull speak. Its message then had been intended for someone other than me, and it had clearly been a warning - which Mr Hendon had ignored - to his ultimate cost.

***

The vicar agreed, and the skull was duly interred in a quiet corner of the graveyard with suitable words to wish its owner a peaceful rest.

I gave Simon and Susan a very brief version of my visit to Mrs Hendon with no mention of strange voices.

To date we have had no further trouble.

JML
8/2/2007

⊰ **CHARITY** ⊱

𝒦enneth Baker had just made love to Charity Brindly and was hating himself. It wasn't the act itself that was the source of his disgust, that had been the sweetest of all he had experienced. Neither was it the girl, Charity was a delight - someone he could easily fall in love with. He was in fact now all too aware of deep stirrings in his heart.

No, it was the manner of the seduction which filled him with self loathing. And he had blown any chance of establishing a proper relationship with her.

***

At the tender age of nineteen Charity was regarded by absolutely everyone who knew her as a thoroughly nice young person. She had everything it takes to qualify for this universal accolade. Well brought-up with impeccable manners her intellect and natural abilities had already seen her leave university with a good degree. Attractive in a gentle, unassuming way, she was also blessed with a mischievous sense of humour, often demonstrated by her ready musical laugh. With sparkling eyes and fresh skin she was a picture of youthful health. Dark brown hair framed a face that was always alive with curiosity. And of those things in life which interested her, and there were many, she was intensely passionate.

Males who met Charity for the first time were unsure which was her most alluring feature, her smile or her gorgeous figure of which she appeared to be unaware.

Now Charity had a unique defence against unwanted attentions from members of the opposite sex - she seemed to be so innocent as to be untouchable, and because of this she left the seat of learning without ever having had full relationship. In this aspect of life she was truly untutored. And this in spite of having a wide circle of friends both men and girls.

She lived at home with devoted parents who were justifiably proud of their only child of whom they hoped would present them with a suitable son in law and grandchildren.

After university she took a job as a buyer for a large chain of pharmacists, and after the initial training courses settled in well.

The company's staff numbered about fifty roughly equally divided between the sexes, most of whom were single.

As you may guess, feelings about Charity were starkly polarised. Most of the women were suspicious of her aura of innocence whilst at the same time being envious of her good looks. The men on the other hand found her immensely attractive but felt themselves somewhat intimidated by her invisible screen of untouchability.

In the steamy office environment both men and women for their various less than wholesome reasons secretly plotted to remove Charity's unsullied armour. Unknowingly our Charity was the main topic of discussion amongst both men and women. Had she known she would have been both surprised and upset.

Into this maelstrom stepped Ken.

He joined the outfit sometime after Charity and so had no inkling as to these local feelings which continued to boil away beneath the normal office veneer of work and everyday chatter.

Now Ken was as worldly as Charity was not. He had had several amatory relationships which were more of a friendly nature than they were serious. These had all ended amicably and he remained uncommitted.

He had never had any trouble attracting admirers, as his devil may care personality was complemented by severely masculine good looks. He had a rich sense of humour and often enjoyed a good joke against himself. He was well liked and considered to be harmless. His problem was - his reputation with the ladies was well known.

Ken loved life and had just bought himself a new bright red and very fast sports car.

He was a good man. If he had one fault it was that he treated life and his relationships in a light-hearted manner not inclined to take anything too seriously.

It was this tendency to frivolity which eventually let him down. It made him all too vulnerable, and came close to breaking the hearts of two good people.

***

The nominal leader of the female pack was a miserable piece of good for nothing who had not a single one of Charity's fine qualities and who was determined to see the angel fall from grace. Beth Rider was not a pleasant person.

But Beth was too clever to be seen as the perpetrator, and when Ken arrived she decided that he was ready-made for the part, and immediately set to work.

Firstly she invited the all too gullible Ken into her intimate circle of friends, most of whom harboured some feelings of jealousy towards our Charity. Then when they had gained Ken's confidence she led the way to Charity's demise.

Given Ken's well known weaknesses the task proved easier than Beth had anticipated.

She hinted to Ken that Charity was interested in him, even suggesting that she would probably be willing to entertain him completely. In these broad hints she was reinforced by the others. It soon became the main topic of every coffee break and every lunchtime get together.

At first Ken's natural respect for Charity's obvious wholesome innocence held him back, but eventually he found he had a strong desire and real feelings for her.

The turning point came when just Ken and Beth were having an after work drink together, and leaning close to him Beth said -

'You know what Ken? You will be doing her a favour. Look upon it as an act of Charity.'

Ken chuckled. 'OK but she may be unwilling.'

'Don't worry we've all got faith in you,' Beth replied.

And so the plot was hatched.

Charity, unused to intense seduction was flattered by Ken's attention, but soon found that she really liked this happy-go-lucky character and her sense of mischief gave her feelings of sheer fun.

GEMSTONE and other fateful tales

Ken's natural abilities did the rest and he and Charity were soon regarded as an item.

And unexpectedly they fell in love. Deeply and totally.

Eventually their feelings were expressed physically to their mutual satisfaction -which is where this tale began.

***

But this happy result was definitely not part of Beth's plan. Her whole intent had been usurped and her pleasure in Charity's demise thwarted. She was not happy and hit on a way to wreck this cosy twosome.

Her plan was wicked.

She arranged to meet Charity 'To tell her something she thought Charity aught to know about Ken.'

When they were settled with drinks and she felt she had Charity's interest she stuck the knife right in - and it went home.

'You know Ken only made love to you because we put him up to it,' she began. Then those devastating words - 'We told him it would be an act of Charity!'

Charity was completely taken aback and at first refused to believe it, but eventually Beth's obvious sincerity won her over, and doing her best to hide her tears she got up and left.

Ken was shocked and hurt by Charity's subsequent frigidity. She refused to talk to him and avoided him as best she could. Ken was puzzled and distraught.

It seemed to be all over and Beth was gleeful.

***

Now Beth had her own lover. He was employed at the same place but he was not one of Beth's group. Sid was a clean living chap, a keen sportsman he loved the outdoor life. It was common knowledge that he and Beth would settle down together as soon as they could find somewhere to live.

Sid was different from Beth in that he had a strong sense of right and wrong, a fact that Beth underestimated as she gloatingly told him of her involvement in splitting up Ken and Charity. Sid said nothing, and kept his deep feelings of disgust from Beth, determined as he was to have it out with Ken whom he knew slightly and whom he liked.

Ken opened his heart when Sid tackled him. As a result Sid determined two things - one, that Ken loved Charity and his feelings for her were genuine, and second the real source of all this unhappiness was his own Beth.

And he determined to sort it.

He arranged to meet Ken and Charity in an out of town pub where they would be uninterrupted. He listened to them both and realised again that Beth was to blame.

He then told them of Beth's role in it all.

Sid looked back as he left and smiled at the sight of two very happy people holding hands and gazing into each other's eyes with fondness and love.

He sighed sadly as he was not looking forward to his next task - he knew he had to tackle Beth.

***

When Beth observed the way Ken and Charity now looked at one another with love written in every glance, she knew that something had gone dreadfully amiss with her little plot, but she had no idea what.

Her phone went and it was Sid asking her to join him at the local after work. Totally unaware of what was about to take place Beth arrived early and ordered herself a gin and it. She sat back sipping her drink happy in anticipation of Sid's arrival.

Sid spotted Beth as soon as he entered and to her surprise he came straight across to her table without ordering his usual pint.

Now Sid was nothing if not a fair man and was prepared to give Beth the benefit of the doubt.

'Why did you tell Charity what you did when you must have know what effect it would have on their relationship?' He asked.

The question and the seriousness with which it was asked shook Beth.

She sat speechless her face getting very red.

'It was unforgivable.' Sid declared, and waited for Beth's reply. When it came it proved to be nearly as shocking to him as was her original action.

Beth exploded.

'What the hell has it got do with you? It was only a joke, where the hell is your sense of humour? Anyway it did no harm,' she added angrily.

Sid waited for her to calm down.

'On the contrary,' he said, 'it made two good people very miserable and all but broke up their relationship. And what's it to do with me - it was me who got them re-united.'

Beth was beside herself with fury.

She stood and hurled the remains of her drink at Sid.

'To hell with you……you straight laced piece of misery…….. We're finished.'

And as Sid wiped away the gin Beth stamped out, leaving Sid looking after her with great sadness in his heart.

He reflected that in all this, his was the one genuine act of charity.

***

Beth left. Ken and Charity were married. Sid met and married a charming acquaintance of Ken and Charity with whom he had become a close friend.

JML
1//4/2007

❖ **THE STALKER** ❖

*O*ver the last few weeks Tandy North had felt her annoyance turn to red hot anger and then to cold fear that coursed through her veins like rivers of ice and pooled round her heart.

At first she suspected she was being followed. Her suspicion became a certainty. And now she knew that she was being stalked.

There could be no other explanation.

It began when she noticed a dark haired rather scruffily dressed man looking in the window of her favourite boutique - an unusual pastime for a man, she thought. But he turned up again wheeling a trolley at the supermarket. And again turning a corner as she got into her car outside the gym. He got on the bus she took in the evening to take her to night school. There he was again, sitting at a corner table in the hotel bar pretending to read a newspaper which was upside down. She got into the habit of looking out for him - and usually there he was pretending to be invisible.

So far he had only sneaked an occasional look at her when he thought she wasn't aware, but she had read of such dreadful happenings to other innocent girls.

Eventually she decided to share her fear with her fiance.

David Brent was a divorced father of two very small children, and having been granted custody was doing his best to bring them up. He had little free time, being both a father and mother and holding down an important job in the city, but managed often enough to spend an evening with Tandy. Sometimes they would book a room in order to express their love for each other in close physical contact. But even on these occasions they would leave before midnight as David had to get back to his offspring.

They knew this situation would not last as they planned on finding a suitable house where they could be a properly married family.

Tandy who lived with her crusty but very loving mother could not wait to join David and spent as much of her free time with him as she could looking at prospective property, she also had a nine to five job in town.

But now there were three of them - Tandy, David, - and the stalker.

Tandy began to be familiar with the stalker's habits. She thought he must have a job since she never saw him during the daytime; but come evening there he would be - at that time of day she could bet on spotting his skulking figure trying to appear to be just another member of the general public.

The situation soon became unbearable. She found that she was looking for him all the time and was even worrying about him when trying to relax at home.

So here she was about to tell David of her concerns.

This step she had avoided so far for fear of what he might do. David worked out regularly and was fast on feet for so big a man. You wouldn't pick a quarrel with David if you wished to get home in one piece.

But she hesitated, and before she told David, the situation boiled over in a truly frightening manner which left them both with years of nightmares, but with their lives intact.

***

It was only a short time after Barbara West married Pedro Badd to become Barbara Badd that she came to realise that he was not the easy going thoughtful person she had first met and fallen in love with.

Pedro's protective nature had slowly turned into a possessive and jealous prison. At the end of each day he would question her every movement often regarding her replies with suspicion and disbelief. When he thought she was not telling the truth he would fly into a rage, offering all manner of threats which left her trembling with fear. Many a time she would sob herself to sleep.

Barbara was a gentle girl who had been raised by loving parents and she was unused to this kind of treatment. What saved her from succumbing to this madness was her little group of women friends whose company she sought whenever she could. A well educated and intelligent person she held down a well paid job as a PA to a company director, and had in addition made friends with several of the female staff.

Pedro disapproved of even these relationships.

The job took Barbara out of Pedro's sight during the day, and she sought every opportunity to spend her evenings with the girls. This latter she enjoyed very much, but these get-togethers were so often spoiled by Pedro's jealous rantings when she got home.

Now Pedro began to notice that Barbara's evenings out were becoming more frequent. He became even more suspicious, especially when he saw how happy she looked when she got home. She also started to return increasingly late.

Then one evening he decided to phone her at the hotel where she had told him she was meeting the girls, and he was told there was no one of that name present. He refused to believe her rational and innocent reason - that they had simply met there and then gone on to a different place.

Pedro was now fully convinced that Barbara was meeting a lover - to him it was the only explanation that met the facts.

One very late evening, when Barbara's fear was such that her story as to where she had been was hesitant and confused, Pedro decided that action was called for.

So he contacted Italian Rab.

Rab, or Rabbit as he was more usually known, was your classic middle man. He survived by a life style that was half way between the law and crime. He had many contacts in both camps, and when arrests or gang battles were around he was always on the side of the good guys. If you wanted drugs, a new passport, money laundered, goods fenced, or protection, Rabbit always knew someone who could provide it - for a price.

His cover was that he ran a one man private detective agency, and for the information he often provided, the law left him alone.

Pedro decided that Rabbit was the very man he needed.

The two men sat sipping drinks in a dark corner of the Old Swan.

'I've got a job for you,' Pedro began.

'I don't do nothin' dirty,' Rabbit warned. He had heard about Pedro.

'Should be an easy one for you, if you're up to it.'

'Could cost a bit, I'm quite busy.'

'It's easy, my wife's having it off with another feller. I want you to follow her, find out where they meet, and tell me so that I can surprise them at it.'

Rabbit sat back and looked at Pedro. He thought he knew what would happen next and was not sure he wanted to be involved. After some thought he decided to make the price prohibitively high, and stated it.

'OK,' said Pedro, and the job was on.

Pedro withdrew a photograph from his pocket and handed it over. Rabbit saw a nice looking woman with a distinctive hairstyle, which she wore coiled up neatly and pinned in position at the back of her head.

A wad of notes change hands, and Pedro told Rabbit where he was most likely to find Barbara. They agreed he would report every other day by phone.

Everything was now set.

The fates however, still had one more card to play - and the results would be terrifying.

The lives of innocent people were about to be placed on the scales.

***

Now it was that Rabbit was not the most intelligent of men, his survival to date was more by good fortune than the use of a keen wit.

He duly arrived at the appointed hostelry and almost immediately spotted a woman with that unusual hairstyle. This was easy he thought, and failed to check with the photograph that this was not Pedro's wife but our Tandy who the fates had decided should meet her man at this very same place.

Rabbit saw them go upstairs, and satisfied with an easy night's work, he left. Had he stayed he would have seen Barbara arrive a little later with her clutch of girl friends.

As a result of his report, Pedro asked for two things - for Rabbit to continue surveillance - and a fully working hand gun, complete with ammunition.

A gun!

Rabbit was frightened, this was outside his rules for self preservation.

Pedro offered very good money.

Rabbit agreed.

The following weeks saw Rabbit trailing Tandy, noting her meetings with David and believing that the lady was Barbara sneaking clandestine meetings with her lover duly reported these back to Pedro.

Barbara continued her evenings out with the girls coincidentally on those same evenings as our Tandy's.

Pedro, seething with pent up fury, pressed Rabbit to come up with the gun.

Fate hesitated.

Rabbit was seriously worried about the gun. Doing a bit on the edge of crime, as it were, was one thing - but being party to murder was another. He was nearly sick with worry - but the money was too tempting and eventually he came up with the goods.

They met out of town by the canal.

'Got it?' Pedro asked.

Rabbit said nothing but produced a piece of rolled-up cloth which he unravelled to reveal an automatic pistol.

'Ammo?'

'It's loaded,' Rabbit replied.

Money changed hands, and Rabbit hurried away in case Pedro decided to try a practice firing.

A couple of days later they met again.

Rabbit told Pedro where and when, and handed over a room key he had copied after leaning heavily on the desk clerk.

A terrible thing was now afoot, and nothing could stop it.

***

The day arrived, and later that evening Tandy and David were in their hired room relaxing on the big double bed after an energetic demonstration of their love. Tandy felt safe in David's strong arms and she even forgot about her stalker.

They dosed gently.

Suddenly their peace was shattered.

A key turned in the lock.

In charged a man they had never seen before.

His face was suffused with fury and in his hand was a gun which he pointed at them.

He fired twice, first at one, then the other.

It was point blank range - he couldn't possibly miss.

The noise of the shots was deafening.

Then to Pedro's astonishment, what should have been a pair of bloody corpses sat up and stared at him with eyes full of fear - he was still waving the gun about.

'Who the hell are you?' Pedro shouted at the girl.

Tandy was too shaken to reply.

Then, realising several things at once Pedro took advantage of the confusion as the place filled with people demanding to know what the row was all about - he scarpered.

Back outside his house, Pedro sat shaking uncontrollably in his car trying to sort things out in his mind.

In substituting blanks for live rounds Rabbit had certainly saved him from committing murder. Rabbit it seemed had been following some strange woman instead of Pedro's wife whom he, Pedro, had actually attempted to kill, along with her lover.

As there was nothing to connect him with the other couple he was probably safe from prosecution.

But above all, it was more than probable that Barbara was innocent after all. And with this thought at the front of his mind he decided to give her the benefit of the doubt. He even began to feel guilty about the way he had treated her.

He sat for sometime longer to let his heart settle down, and wondered vaguely why Barbara had not appeared. He felt a longing for her that he hadn't experienced for a long time.

The house was in darkness and felt cold when he eventually let himself in.

Of Barbara there was no sign, he checked every room.

He next went to the cabinet to pour himself a drink and there propped against the whisky bottle was an envelope.

Inside was a short note - it said:-

Dear Pedro,

I loved you once but I no longer do. Your suspicion of me has driven me to this action for which I am sorry. You must know in your heart that I have never been unfaithful to you either in thought or deed in all the time we have been together.
Please do not try to find me, I have gone to live with one of my (lady) friends who has a place in a warmer climate. I have changed my name and wish to be left alone to get on with my life.

I wish you well

There was no goodbye, and it was unsigned.

***

Tandy and David often had nightmares about their frightening experience but thankfully they never knew how close they came to death. They concluded that the man with the gun had just been out to frighten someone.
Coincidentally, and mysteriously Tandy's stalker was never seen by her again - much to her intense relief.

JML
18/2/2007

◈ **HOPE** ◈

*I*t might be considered that one aspect which makes for a successful couple is that they should have much in common.

But in the case of young Barry Coates and Belinda McNairn they were so much alike they very nearly didn't make it, even though they were attracted to each other from the start.

Both our friends attended local single sexed schools, left at the same time and started at the same provincial university on the same day. Up until then they had never clapped eyes on one another.

They both came from good homes and each had a younger sibling of the opposite sex.

To describe one is also to describe the other. Shy in the extreme, preferring gentle environments and gentle pursuits. Honest and sincere to a fault. Blessed with natural good looks and with a gift for neatness in everything.

They had sharing rooms on campus (obviously not with each other) and were keen to succeed.

Probably the only significant difference between them was that Barry was studying History and Art, whereas Belinda was doing Geology and Art. An unusual combination this latter - but there we have it, that's as it was.

Now you are probably thinking 'what a boring pair', but you would be very wrong. They each had a terrific sense of humour, and liking for adventure, and as a result were popular and well liked.

To date their inherent shyness had eclipsed any thoughts they had of an intimate relationship with a member of the opposite sex. It wasn't that they each hadn't considered it, they had, but contemplation was one thing - action was another.

Barry had never asked a girl out, whilst Belinda had studiously avoided being asked.

None of this made either of them unhappy, they simply lived in the hope that something would come along in due course. But so far nothing had.

Now it happens that every now and then fate brings two individuals together who recognise immediately that they are meant for each other. They usually roll up their sleeves and get on with it (whatever 'it' might be). But not if you are either Barry or Belinda.

Under different tutors, even for their common study, art, they did not meet for some time. But then one fine day in May they were both scheduled to be on a coach trip to the local art gallery to view and discuss their collection of European, nineteenth century paintings.

Barry hoped he might get to sit next to a nice girl with whom he might strike up a conversation. Belinda hoped for a bloke. Neither was lucky.

But all as yet was not lost.

As the group was escorted round by the tutor Barry noticed this very pleasant quiet young lady who asked hardly any questions but looked at the paintings with intense interest, her face often lit by a gentle smile which shared itself with the occasional intense frown. His heart began to entertain feelings quite new to Barry who had no idea what they meant.

Belinda had not failed to notice Barry and was starting to wonder about him.

They both hoped to be sitting together on the return trip.

No such luck. The attendant took a while finding Barry's coat, and last on board he was seated a long way from Belinda.

From this you might think that a small seed of hope had been sown in both their hearts - and you would be right.

But suitable follow-up action was not forthcoming.

It is true that from that time on Barry thought of Belinda with longing but was so afraid of being rejected by her, or even worse making a fool of himself that he actually avoided any chance of an accidental meeting. She on the other hand badly wanted Barry to speak to her but was afraid of not matching up to his requirements, and was therefore also trying to keep out of his way.

A strange situation this, don't you think? Here were two people hoping that some kind of magic would draw them together and yet afraid to make it happen.

It looked very much as if they were to remain apart for ever.

And yet they had hope.

Fate did its best, and there were several near misses.

They both attended the first year end of term dance, each being cajoled into it by a group of well intentioned friends - so what happened?

Barry was commandeered for the whole evening by a nice rather buxom young lady who saw the chance of a bedtime romp with him mistaking his natural politeness for real interest. She was quite miffed when at the end of the evening Barry did not come up to scratch, with not even so much as a goodnight kiss.

Poor Barry spent the whole time trying to catch glimpses of Belinda as she was whirled around the floor by a succession of would be suitors.

The situation remained unchanged over the term break, and for both our friends hope was renewed as the second year got under way.

It started well.

Belinda's art tutor was taken ill and was temporarily confined to his home, and both groups were taken over by Barry's chap. Thus relative close proximity was unavoidable. It should have been great but remember, this was Barry and Belinda.

Both were so afraid of looking foolish in front of the other that each developed a kind of frosty remoteness not just to each other but to the rest of the group and also their long suffering tutor.

One dreadfully embarrassing incident occurred when Barry was asked to render a criticism of Belinda's work - you can imagine his chagrin.

He stood behind Belinda studying her canvass for so long without a word that even the other students started to make restless comments and the tutor was forced to intervene.

GEMSTONE and other fateful tales

Student - 'Come on Barry get a move on, I don't want to be late for tomorrows rugby match.'

Student - 'I think he's fallen asleep. Let's not wake him he may be having an erotic dream.'

Tutor - 'Barry, valid criticism is an essential part of the course, it's as important to the artist as it is to you. So, when you're ready can we have your views please?'

Barry - 'Sorry, I think.....em.......that......em.......'

He managed eventually to say that he thought the choice of colours was excellent but was not quite so sure of the overall impact.

When pushed to say why, he gave a long winded neutral statement which left all at a loss to comprehend.

The tutor was annoyed because he knew Barry was normally a very forthright critic, but he didn't know about Barry and Belinda, did he?

From this and other similar instances it soon became well known to the whole fraternity that Barry and Belinda were quite keen on each other, but were too afraid to do more than look with those sad hopeful eyes.

Fortunately for the hesitant pair fate had not quite given up.

Belinda's brother, who was just one year younger than she, attended a St Valentine's Day dance with his mates at the local civic centre. They were having a great time at the bar when a crowd of unescorted girls entered. As the lads moved in he found himself with a charming young lady of about the same age as himself, and who seemed somewhat different than the rest. For a start she was more intelligent having well formed opinions on a wide variety of subjects. He also soon found that she had a wicked sense of humour and even risked pulling his leg, the novelty of which he found he enjoyed.

Roger was a quick lad and realised that Rose also liked what she saw in him.

Unlike Barry and Belinda these two knew what they wanted and soon became a pair.

They took to going out together to the theatre, to music venues, the cinema, and even trips away - they were both keen walkers and were specially fond of the Lake District.

The fates smiled.

And hope lived anew.

These two had booked seats for a much sought after comedian's appearance at their favourite place of entertainment and were very much looking forward to it.

But they were not destined to go.

There was a spate of flu going round and being close when one got it so did the other.

Roger in an uncharacteristic fit of generosity gave his ticket to Belinda.

And Rose presented hers to her brother.

***

The night of the event arrived.

Belinda wore her special occasion gown and it has to be said that she looked terrific - a head turner if their ever was one. She was a bit nervous about being on her own but Robert assured her that she would be OK - the venue was quite posh, and when asked, he told her that Rose had given her ticket to her brother who he thought was a pleasant enough chap.

And thus it was that Belinda climbed out of the taxi, purchased a program, and was escorted to her seat by a charming lady attendant.

The seat beside her was vacant.

She had not been in this theatre before and was so engrossed in taking in her surroundings that she did not see the man before he was seated and when she did they both got a shock.

Belinda was looking into Barry's eyes.

***

You will no doubt have guessed way back that Barry was Rose's elder brother.

After the show, which was excellent, our two friends went for drinks. The ice was well and truly broken and they just never stopped talking.

Their relationship came as a surprise to Roger and Rose but not to the members of the college who breathed sighs of relief, and actually cheered them the following day when they arrived together.

JML
26/2/2007

❧ INVASION ☙

*I*t was a real brain teaser. Not even the old hands at the local nick could remember seeing anything like it. It was the main topic of conversation in the village. At the church, in the pub, in the shops, the hairdressers, in fact everywhere that people met, it was discussed. And they railed at the police for failing to solve the mystery. The local news sheet laid the blame fairly and squarely at the Chief Constable's door, and he was not only depressed at his failure but had no idea as to what action to take other than that which he had already done. He knew his job was on the line.

But it didn't stop.

Nothing of consequence ever happened in the Rural District of Upper Trenwich, but now the atmosphere of peace and calm had, over the last twelve months, been shattered by a series of break-ins.

Only big houses standing in their own grounds had so far been entered. Nothing strange about that, but what was a puzzle to everyone was that in each case nothing, absolutely nothing was taken.

Jewellery - untouched. Loose cash - left where it was. Artwork - not even a mark left on it. Silver - still where it had been laid.

And yet in every instance there were clear signs of a break-in, a forced window, a broken lock, and in one case a double glazed window smashed. But apart from this each place had been left totally undisturbed.

It was impossible to understand.

There were theories of course, plenty of them.

The postman's view was popular. He reckoned it was the action of someone simply seeking a thrill, an adrenalyn lift.

A few of the house owners affected thought it was someone looking for drugs and not finding any simply left..

Some thought the culprit must have been disturbed before they had got going.

But in the police station they dealt in facts.

A very depressed Chief Constable stood looking at the incident board on which was displayed a huge space largely devoid of facts.

There were some things common to all eight cases so far investigated. The board showed them -

1. Took place at night.
2. Owners were out or away.
3. Nothing taken. Or disturbed (except 4.)
4. Evidence of drawers having been searched.
5. No finger or foot prints.
6. No vehicle tracks.
7. No day or date pattern.
8. No unaccounted for visitors.
9. Owners unrelated (business or family)
10. No similar MO's on the police data base.

He was staring at an almost complete blank.

But he wasn't about to give up. It was not his way. This problem had a rational explanation, of that he was sure, and he was determined to solve it.

Before he could decide what action to take, a couple of local councillors and the county MP set up a press meeting at which he was invited to answer questions put to him by the village residents. He had no choice but to attend.

***

In spite of the wet conditions on the evening of the event, the community centre was packed. (The vicar wished he could attract so many to his church on Sundays). At the table facing the audience was the Chief Constable, and in a show of solidarity, were the MP and two well known members of the local council. They looked unhappy people.

When the doors were eventually closed the MP called for quiet and got it.

'Well we all know why we are here,' he began, 'we have been suffering from a series of break-ins by a person or persons unknown. So far in spite of diligent policing -' Several members of the audience jeered. 'the perpetrators are still at large.'

He nodded to the Chief Constable, and continued - 'I now invite Stanley Nailum our police chief to give us an update and to tell us what future action is planned for our safety.'

There was an immediate clamour from the floor.

'We're not safe in our beds!'

'Where are the police when we need them?'

'You'll have to get off your large backsides!'

This last remark raised a laugh as the Chief was himself quite portly.

Into the quiet when it was re-established the Chief spoke with a confidence he did not feel.

'I have to admit that so far we have drawn a complete blank. As in each case nothing was taken and no forensic evidence left by the offender we have precious little to go on. We don't even know what may be the reason for these break-ins.'

'We have checked with the central police files and nothing similar has ever been recorded.'

A voice from the audience shouted - 'So what are you going to do about it, we don't feel safe any more.'

The Chief waited for calm then told them the only thing he could.

'I have requested and received four more constables who together with our own four will maintain a constant nightly patrol - and this will continue until the person responsible is caught. I'm afraid this is all we can hope to do. - nevertheless I am determined to succeed in this matter.'

He paused, then -

'Now if you will permit me I will return to the station to put this plan into action.'

Amidst the rumpus that followed he rose and left the room.

***

And so overnight policing in this quiet very English backwater began. And almost immediately there was a very near miss. Police constable Stan Blake was on patrol. It was damp and cold. Fed up with walking around for nothing and strictly against rules he nipped home for a brew and a bite to eat. Anxious not to be caught out he took a short cut back through the church grounds and the grounds of one of the big houses he was supposed to be guarding.

Quite suddenly and unexpectedly he spotted a dark figure, only just visible in the dusk, reaching up to a ground floor window.

This is it, he thought and raced towards the figure.

Unfortunately in the dark he tripped on a broken branch and fell headlong.

His tumble was heard by the figure which promptly turned and ran even before constable Blake could stand up, which he did painfully having gashed his leg quite badly.

A post mortem was held the next morning at the station where a very embarrassed constable Blake was telling his tale. Most of his colleagues were sympathetic but the Chief was clearly angry.

However Stan Blake did have one fact to offer which simply added to the puzzle.

He was, he said, absolutely certain that the figure was that of a girl.

'And a fit one at that,' he added ruefully.

There were two more successful break-ins, as a result of which the police did elicit one fact, but it was so strange as to add to the mystery rather than solve it.

The perpetrator had searched for only one thing which had been inspected but not removed.

PHOTOGRAPHS.

In spite of these misses, success when it came was as unusual as the break-ins themselves and was not down to the police.

Stella and William Boston owners of one of the big houses had taken a few days to go north to do some shooting on a friend's estate.

They returned home as dawn was breaking having travelled early to miss the traffic.

Whilst William garaged the four by four, Stella produced her key and let herself in.

She passed the open door to the lounge as she made her way to the kitchen and what she saw in there gave her the shock of her life. It was a scene she would never forget.

She just stood and gaped.

Sat at the table, surrounded by a pile of photographs and albums, was a slim girl dressed all in black.

Her head rested on her folded arms on the table, and she was fast asleep.

***

Surprise held Stella.

Then William strode through the front door loudly demanding a cup of tea and breakfast.

The girl stirred and looked up.

A pale but lovely face gazed at Stella.

She said nothing but her sad eyes told of much unhappiness.

'Who the bloody hell.........,' said William looking over Stella's shoulder.

Stella recovered. The girl seemed harmless.

'I'll make us a cup of tea, and then perhaps you will explain yourself.'

The girl began to cry silently.

GEMSTONE and other fateful tales

'This is nonsense,' said William, 'we should call the police.' But he said this without conviction, his curiosity having been roused.

Soon all three were seated at the big dining table sipping from steaming mugs.

Stella took charge.

'First things first,' she began.

'What's your name?'

'Patsy Banner.'

'And how old are you Patsy?'

'Sixteen.'

'Well then Patsy you are in our house and I'm Stella and this is my husband William. So now what in heaven's name are you after?'

Patsy looked down at the table where all but three photographs had been pushed aside, two were quite battered and obviously belonged to Patsy. One of these was of a big house partly visible through some trees, the other was a portrait of a good looking young woman. However the third photo she had extracted from one of the Boston's own albums - it was also a portrait and was of the very same young woman. Although these two pictures were somewhat different the match was unmistakable.

What came next was a shock.

Pointing at the portraits, Patsy said pleadingly -

'Please, this is my mother.'

Stella was shocked, how on earth could this be?

Patsy again -

'Please tell me, who is she?'

'You are holding pictures of my mother's younger sister taken when she was about your age.' Then with a voice full of sadness for what it may mean to Patsy she told her - 'She died of cancer just a few short years after that photograph was taken.'

'It's all right,' said Patsy, 'I knew she must be dead otherwise she would have found me, and she didn't.'

***

And so it was.

Patsy was Stella's niece. Unknown until that day she broke in.

She told the police the whole story.

Living hand to mouth with an elderly lady who cared for her in a block of flats in a run-down suburb of our capital city she had no financial resources of her own. The lady had died and left two photographs with a letter explaining that the portrait was her mother and that she lived in the big house in the photograph in the village of Upper Trenwich. But she thought her mother may now be dead.

The only other information was that her mother had been forced to give her away at birth. Her father had been a soldier and had been killed in action..

As Patsy explained to the police, she could think of no way of finding her family other than comparing her photograph - hence the break-ins.

***

The local press treated Patsy's story sympathetically. No one pressed charges. Stella and William, so far childless, took her in as one of the family - which indeed she was.

***

Strangely Chief Constable Stanley Nailum took all the credit and was commended.

JML
3/3/2007

⊰ **THE MAN WHO DUG** ⊱

I knew 'the man who dug'. After all he did live next door.

In every other respect he was not in the least unusual - except for the fact that he dug.

Albert (Bert) Skinnard moved into his new house about the same time as my wife and I moved into ours.

We met, as neighbours often do, quite often to spend the time of day or to assist in some small task, and I suppose I knew him as well as anyone outside his immediate family.

Bert was then aged about sixty or so, fit and reasonably athletic. With his ever suffering wife Elsie they had a son and a daughter both of whom were married and had themselves six children between them. I said 'between them' because they always visited in a bunch and I never did sort out who belonged to who.

Our estate occupied what had previously been a spread of four odd shaped fields, this had ensured that each house had a very different shape and size of garden. Ours had a small front patch, just enough for a couple of decent rose beds and a very small lawn, and about the same at the back, suitable in fact for an occasional and reluctant gardener.

Bert's house on the other hand had hardly any ground at the front, but was graced with a sweep of about half an acre at the rear. The whole extent of this large back garden was overlooked by us, such that we had a bird's eye view of all that happened there. Not a snail could move without our seeing it.

In those days we all had day jobs, so any outdoor domestic activities were relegated to week-ends and holidays, so that for some months nothing much changed - the view from our windows to the rear remained the same.

Then, one spring day - he began.

We watched fascinated.

Dressed for the occasion in workman-like overalls, Bert appeared with a wheel barrow in which he was transporting a variety of tools and a largish sheet of paper which we guessed was a plan of some kind. He then proceeded to read from the plan and mark out using string and pegs a largish rectangular shape.

What he had started we could only guess at - but started he had.

Had we known we might just have moved out then and there. But we didn't.

The beginning was slow and the effect quite modest.

Grass disappeared from Bert's rectangle together with about six inches of soil which he spread on his small front patch.

Then Bert told me in passing how busy he was at work, so nothing further happened for several weeks and we relegated looking to an occasional glance.

We took a long weekend away to enjoy the benefit of some glorious summer weather and got a shock on our return - Bert's hole was now at least a couple of feet deep. He must have worked like the very devil.

What on earth was he about?

We couldn't guess. And where had all that soil gone?

Now the Skinnards were away themselves and we had no one to ask.

On their return a bronzed Bert with sleeves rolled up appeared and promptly set to work, and we quickly discovered where the soil went. A skip was now parked on the small forecourt of their house with a large plank placed to aid Bert's wheel barrow as he tipped the soil into it. In due course the full skip was taken away and replaced with an empty one.

Bert's hole got deeper.

It was now so deep that it took Bert a much greater effort to fill the barrow for each load, and so the work slowed down.

And then he hit bed rock.

Now the hole was visible over the low garden wall from the road in front of our two houses, and much to our irritation curious passers-by would stop to gaze at Bert in action, and even took to looking at the hole when nothing was happening.

Had we known it then this was only the very beginning.

All summer Bert dug his hole.

Eventually I stopped him one day -

'Bert, I hope you don't mind my asking, but what are you doing in your garden - it's causing a great deal of interest?' I asked.

`Don't worry old chap, this is only Phase One,' he replied. `So you must excuse me I must keep going.' And having cleared that up he returned to the dig.

Phase one! What the hell did he mean?

He then hit a snag. We had a period of very wet weather and Bert's hole filled with water and we saw him gazing forlornly at it as the rain continued to patter the surface of what was now quite a deep pool.

That will stop him we said, but we had reckoned without Bert's determination.

Taking advantage of the next fine spell we watched Bert set up a powerful water pump and fix a strong canvass awning over the work area. The hole was drained, and the digging continued, except that the work was slow as Bert now had to use crow-bar and pick-axe to shift the rock.

Before the autumn turned to winter Bert had replaced the covering with a more substantial wooden structure, and had built concrete steps down to the bottom and was clearly preparing to concrete the sides.

Winter brought digging to a halt, but on fine days a heavily garbed Bert could be seen with plan and tape measure busily marking out god knows what in the hitherto untouched part of his garden.

When we did meet, Bert complained bitterly about the problems he was having from the council brought about by our neighbours raising the matter of what he was doing. And so far they had reassured him and them that he was doing nothing to warrant their interference.

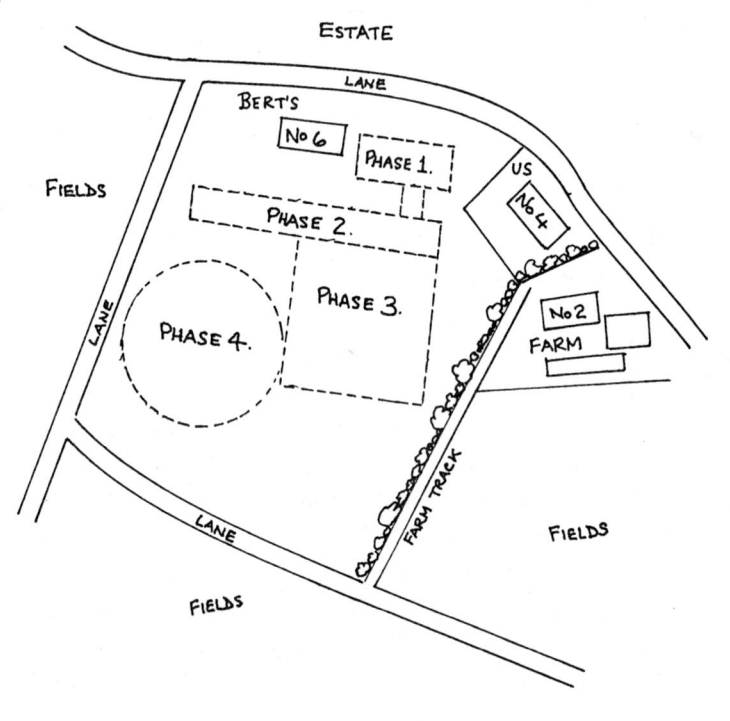

BERT'S GRAND PLAN

The next spring arrived and we soon became aware that what we had seen so far was only a prelude to the main event.

A large trench had appeared which stretched itself across almost the full width of the rear garden, and this time he had covered it with a broad awning so that work could continue in the dry.

And Bert dug on.

'Sorry Bert but just what in heaven's name are you doing now?' I asked as he wheeled a barrow load past me.

'Phase Two!' He declared over his shoulder, and disappeared round the house to where the umpteenth skip was waiting.

However this new effort caused a significant increase in interest. Bert's garden was sandwiched on two sides by a narrow lane and on the third side by a farm track which was also a public right of way. Now on dry days, and at all daylight hours a number of curious heads would appear over the low garden hedge. There was sometimes quite a large crowd and the mobile ice cream van took advantage of the situation to call several times a day especially at weekends. It was rumoured in the local pub that people even came from the next villages just to look.

Bert refrained from digging when the grandchildren arrived and even invented games for them which made full use of his trenches, and they loved it, they were especially good at inventing games of their own.

In terms of entertainment the holes were a great success.

All this slowed Bert down and phase two took the best part of five years before Bert moved on to Phase Three.

Phase Three.

This proved to be yet another giant hole. It adjoined phase two and was at least as big as the two previous phase added together.

But it remained a mystery what it was all for.

The debate took much time and discussion at the Miner's Arms, and as no one really knew the answer, it was anyone's guess.

'I reckon he's preparing for the next war,' this from the postman.

'Naw, taint gonna be much use against atomic bombs,' the milkman pointed out.

'It might if he reaches Australia,' returned the postman.

This was greeted by laughter.

'Perhaps he knows there is buried treasure down there,' surmised the teacher.

'Well if there is, he hasn't found it yet,' chipped in the carpenter.

'I think he is responding to Aliens who are telling him what to do,' said the librarian who in the opinion of most people present suffered from too much reading.

'If aliens land here I reckon they must be lost,' mine host pointed out.

More laughter.

'Well whatever he's up to it's good for business, it's brought quite a lot of visitors, so I hope he keeps going.' this from the shopkeeper.

'I'll bet a tenner he gives up before next year,' the barman offered.

But before anyone could take him on, Bert himself entered.

'- and he's also a pretty useful batsman,' continued the barman.

And sighs of relief could be heard.

It had been agreed that when Bert was present his activities in his garden would not be mentioned in the hope of teasing him into divulging his secret. But so far this strategy had failed.

Phase Three being on an altogether grander scale took Bert a further ten years and his age was starting to tell. He was now in his late seventies, retired, and although reasonably fit the continuous work had its effect and he suffered from aching joints

I was sympathising with him about his aches and pains one day when he surprised me by announcing that he was about to start Phase Four. But before I could ask him, he had apologised and toddled off.

Then one day we had a visitor. I answered the door to Elsie who stood there clearly trying to withhold her tears.

Seated with a stiff drink she poured out her heart to us.

She was desperately worried about Bert she told us. His health was failing and in spite of all her pleadings he wouldn't hear a word about giving up his digging. She was sure he would kill himself. Maybe we could get him to stop or at least ease off a bit.

'I promise you I will do my best, but we have no idea what he is trying to build, what are the holes for?' I asked.

'Do you know, I have no idea,' Elsie replied. 'I've asked him many times, but he just will not say. I hardly see him from one day to the next. When it rains he works in the boxroom on what he calls `the Plan'.' She dabbed her eyes.

Even though we promised to do our best to get Bert to stop, we had little confidence in being able to do so.

I did try.

'Bert old chap, we are all concerned about you. Should you be doing all this hard work? What the devil is it all for anyway. You know Elsie is worried sick that you will be ill and she doesn't want to loose you.' I had made my pitch, and could do no more.

'It's nice of you to be concerned,' he replied, 'but I just want to finish this phase then I might think about taking it easy for a while. So thanks again my friend, but now you must excuse me, I have quite a bit to do today.'

But whatever were his real intensions, he continued to dig.

And with the inevitable result.

It was only a few days after my conversation with him that Bert did not appear for his evening meal.

Elsie hammered on our door , and when I opened it she almost fell into my arms. She was ashen and shaking.

'Will you go and see?' Was all she could get out.

She showed me through he house to the rear door. Once there she stood and pointed out to where Bert's constructions and holes were laid out.

I had no idea where to look and was fearful as to what I might find.

I found him at the bottom of what I think he called phase three which was a large squarish hole about six feet deep. His barrow was tipped on one side having fallen off the ramp which led down to the floor, and huddled beside it, flat on his back, was Bert. His face was a deadly pasty colour and his eyes were closed.

The ramp was steep and slippery, but I made it to the bottom where I ascertained that Bert was still breathing, but was not answering me. With no knowledge of first-aid I hot footed it back to the house and dialled 999.

The ambulance arrived after I spent about fifteen minutes trying to comfort a distraught Elsie helped now by my wife who had rushed round to help.

The medics were great. I don't know how they did it but they stretchered Bert out of his hole, through the house and into the ambulance.

Bert came round briefly, but it was clear from the lads that there was little anyone could do.

It was Elsie who asked the question, in an anguished voice.

'Bert, my love what was all that digging about?'

He opened his eyes, and a weak smile momentarily lit is face.

Then in a voice that could barely be heard he said -

'It gave me something to do.' They were his last words on this earth.

JML
9/3/2007

❖ **MURDER - THE ONLY SALVATION** ❖

*V*ery gradually and painfully he began to acknowledge that he was waking up, and he dreaded it. As his mind started to clear, a sinking, leaden feeling began to squeeze his insides.

He was absolutely terrified.

For what seemed the hundredth time he wondered what prison was really like, and if he had the stamina to survive the years. He had no options left. He would have to endure whatever punishment the law demanded.

However justified, he had committed the ultimate crime.

He had deliberately, and in cold blood, taken the life of another human being.

He closed his eyes and tried to shut out the dawning day, but the vivid memory of what had taken place and what led up to it would not go away.

The crisis had arisen slowly.

Some fifteen years ago at the age of fifty-five Stanley Wholewood had been made redundant from his job with a large international engineering company. They needed to downsize they said. After many applications and a few interviews he struck lucky and landed a design position with a smaller but very go-ahead family business.

The next ten years were the happiest and most rewarding of his career, but it did not last. He was offered a management post which did not appeal to him but which he had little choice but to accept. He joined a team of five, all of whom he got on with extremely well - the problem was his new boss.

Right from the outset the boss, Dick De-range, made it clear that this appointment was not his decision, and the sooner he got rid of the newcomer the better.

It was also abundantly clear that he did not like Stanley, who never did find out why, although he suspected that Dick thought he was well in with higher management and might one day replace him.

As his boss he did everything possible to be-little him, taking full advantage of exploiting any small errors he thought he might have made; and even blaming Stanley for his own mistakes.

Of course as boss he claimed all Stanley's successes as his own.

Why put up with this treatment you may ask?

Well, with a fair sized house, a wonderful and loyal wife, two children each with at least another year to do at university and an expectation of expensive holidays abroad, you can see why he was desperate to keep this job.

Since he found that Stanley did not intend to leave voluntarily Dick began to use every trick in the book, and one or two new ones.

There was one task that involved someone going round all eighteen associated companies gathering data which then had to be consolidated into a comprehensive report.

As this meant being away for home and living in hotels for a considerable period it was universally disliked by the team, so they devised a rota to share the job fairly between them.

This worked extremely well, but one day `dirty' Dick decided to scrap the rota and give the job solely to Stanley.

It goes without saying that Dick took full advantage of Stanley's frequent absences to make the most mischief for him that he possibly could. On Stanley's return the rest of the team would warn him of anything he needed to put right.

If Dick's intention was to drive Stanley to do something drastic which would cost him his job then he was succeeding.

Worry began to affect Stanley's health, and this was seized on by Dick who loudly announced that Stanley was ill, and it was affecting his work.

Stanley worried what higher management's view of his work really was. He worried what would happen to his family if he got the sack. He worried in case the quality of his work really was suffering. But above all he worried what devilish plan that bastard Dick would come up with next.

Not only was Stanley's work affected but it had begun to spoil his home life, turning him into a more and more grumpy, unreasonable and unpleasant husband and father.

He finally decided that this couldn't go on, the next time Dick would pull a really bad trick he would do something drastic.

Then, in an uncharacteristic fit of rage Stanley found himself wanting to cause Dick some physical injury. This was most unlike Stanley but he felt that he had to assuage some of the wrong Dick had meted out to him over the years.

He realised that he would be number one suspect - but by now he had had enough - he could not take any more - it had to be physical and brutal. Desperation had taken over.

Then one cold winter's day came that final straw.

The firm announced that there had to be a reduction of staff which meant some early retirements, or for the lucky ones - redundancy with its excellent financial reward.

Unfortunately Stanley could not afford either, he was desperate for those few extra years of employment, and at his age he was not likely to get another lucrative post.

But Dick was in his worst gloating mood.

'Well now, the management have asked me for my recommendations - and guess who is top of my list to go?' He said with a huge grin on his fat pasty face.

So this was it then, thought Stanley - now he had nothing to loose.

Stanley was no longer master of his own actions.

***

Dick's usual route home took him through the local woods. These were a playground for kids, walkers with dogs and keep fit fanatics during the day, but were largely deserted in the hours of darkness.

It was only last night but Stanley could hardly believe what he had done.

His memory of it was vivid.

He had left work well before Dick and with no clear plan, and had hidden himself by the path through the woods that he knew Dick usually took. And as he waited a red rage seized him, blinding him to all rational thought.

Then Dick's hated figure appeared in the gloom and without being aware of it Stanley found himself with a large branch in his fist. He stepped out behind Dick and raised the branch. But as he brought it down on Dick's head, Dick turned and looked directly at Stanley.

It was a glancing blow and Dick turned and started to run, but he was not a fit man and Stanley soon caught him up and struck him again.

This time Dick fell and Stanley beat him again and again on the head until he was sure that life was extinct.

Without a backward look, but with a great sense of release Stanley made his way home. As he came to the bridge over the river he flung the branch he was still clutching into the swirling dark water and watched it as the current took it rapidly from sight. It would be far out at sea by dawn.

As the day broke, the vivid memory of his crime filled his horrified mind. He could not believe that he, a loving husband and father could do such a thing. As he shaved and dressed he trembled continuously, and at breakfast found that he could not look his family in their eyes, and unusually he did not join in their breakfast time conversation.

Then his wife Jean went to answered a knock at the door, and ushered two policemen into the lounge where they each took a seat. Then with absolute confidence that there was nothing amiss that Stanley could not deal with, returned to do the clearing up.

As Stanley entered they stood. A tall slim sergeant and a young PC looked grim.

'Good morning. Please do sit,' said Stanley as he seated himself.

'What can I do for you gentlemen?'

'Good morning sir, I am Sergeant Knowles and this is PC Pennington, he will take notes if you don't mind.

This is it, thought Stanley, and nearly passed out with fear.

'I gather you are employed by Air Frame Industries?'

'That's correct.'

'And you are well acquainted with a Mr er De-range?'

'Yes, he is my immediate boss.'

'Quite so! Would you mind telling me what time you left your place of work sir?'

They are always polite when it's serious, thought Stanley.

'It was about six thirty, I think,' he replied.

'And was Mr De-range still there when you left?'

'Yes I believe he was.'

The sergeant paused and looked mournful, and then -

'What kind of mood would you say he was in when you last saw him?'

What the devil was he getting at, thought Stanley?

'Well as far as I could tell he seemed to be his usual self. But why do you ask?'

Again the policeman paused, and seemed to gather himself.

Then came the words Stanley could not believe, and would never, ever, forget.

'I'm afraid I have some very bad news for you sir. Mr De-range was found hanged at the factory early this morning. He had committed suicide. On his desk we found a note which explained why he had resorted to such drastic action, and a letter addressed to his wife, which we have yet to deliver.'

'I am shocked, and very sorry indeed,' replied Stanley, he could not believe it and felt they must have made a mistake. 'Are you sure?' He asked.

'Very sure sir, the body has been identified by several people.'

Stanley's mind was in a whirl. The man whose brains he had smashed in, had hanged himself, how on earth could this be?

'Why?' Stanley uttered the one word.

'Apparently he had just been sacked.'

Stanley simply gaped. Then a thought occurred to him.

'Tell me why you have come to me?' He asked.

'Two reasons sir, firstly you were probably the last person to see him alive, and secondly Mr De-range's manager had named you as the new departmental head, that is De-range's replacement.'

Bloody hell, thought Stanley - one minute a murderer and the next a boss. He gave up puzzling, stood up thanked the officers and saw them out.

He entered the kitchen, sat down and hesitatingly told his wife just what the policeman had said. He should have been elated but found himself close to tears. He could not see how it could be. In his mind's eye he could still visualise De-range's body on the grass with its head bashed in.

'You know?' He said. 'I'm very, very tired.'

'I'm really not surprised,' she said. 'You had a terrible night, waving your arms about and shouting. You seemed to be hitting something or someone. I had to sleep in the spare room - it went on for ages. I can't imagine what you were dreaming about.'

But Stanley knew all too well.

JML
12/3/2007

⚢ **THE WAY THAT MONEY GOES ROUND** ⚣

*S*ten fingered with satisfaction the two coins in her pocket as she climbed down the stone steps of the seventh fort on the Big Wall. A quick look round to ensure she would not be seen, and with her cloak over her head to stave off some of the rain, she made her way back to her home and family. Arius Augustus was a man not difficult to please, the usual trouble was the it took all Sten's arts to get him roused. Once that achieved, it was all over very quickly. Today had been no exception and she considered it was easy money.

What puzzled Sten was why he had chosen her when there were more attractive and younger women available. It wasn't that she was ugly, with a good figure and warm welcoming smile she was nevertheless a mature mother of six children, and it showed.

But these Romans were far from home and clearly missing their women.

They still had ten miles of construction to complete the wall, and Sten wondered vaguely if the Romans would leave when it was complete. It was well known that the cold climate did not please most of the foreigners and the everyday rumours were of imminent departure.

Sten was intent on not being seen because although everyone she knew did it - it was nevertheless forbidden (by both sides) to mix with the foreigners, that is aside from traders and work gangs.

Fights between marauding gangs from the north were thankfully becoming less frequent, demonstrating the walls deterrent effect, and times here were now a great deal more peaceful.

***

It was vital to Sten's survival that no-one, especially her ever loving husband, discovered what she had been about. She therefore needed to get rid of the tell-tale coins as soon as possible. With this in mind she made her way to the encampment where most of the local workforce lived, and called on the man who supplied meat to those who could afford it.

Benk took her away from prying eyes and viewed the coins greedily. He too would like to sample Sten's favours but money was more exchangeable. They agreed that for one coin he would provide four day's worth of venison, a rare treat for Sten's family; and he would take the second coin as credit against future provisions.

Sten then made her way home clutching a parcel of hide in which was a nice slice of meat, and as she struggled along the boggy path she dreamt of the pleasure her husband would give her after they had fed. He might have had his suspicions but good food was hard to come by in this poor district and a real feast.

Notices had been posted along the wall of a forthcoming gladiatorial fight, the main event of which was a battle between the local Roman hero and victor of many such fights, and a local strong man who belonged to Arius Augustus. These opponents were listed to be the tournament's last event.

The day was fine and the arena was crowded as Benk slid surreptitiously to the side of his usual betting agent. He was offered odds of 'four to one on' for a clean win by the gladiator and 'evens' on the local man.

They had to be careful as only the Romans were allowed to bet openly. So Benk merely showed his two coins and his bet on the local man was accepted.

As a contest it looked uneven. The foreigner was slightly built reaching no higher than the other's shoulders, whereas the slave's strength was written in his bulging muscular limbs and torso. Against this giant the other had the advantage of having survived many such duals. It was a case of the swift and cunning versus brute force.

After the blood and guts of the previous fights these two eventually faced each other armed only with a shield and short Roman stabbing sword.

Half an hour into the battle and the Gladiator had the edge having inflicted several deep wounds on his opponent but without as yet defeating him. It seemed only a matter of time and the crowd of mostly paid soldiers were loudly encouraging their hero of many fights to finish it off. Benk resigned himself to loosing his precious two coins.

But they reckoned without fate.

Executing a smart turn the gladiator stumbled. He remained on his feet but exposed. The giant didn't hesitate, he threw away his shield and sword, and clasping both fists together he brought them down on the neck of the Roman.

The whole arena heard his spine snap and he dropped dead at the other's feet.

The crowd went wild. Benk collected his winnings, two more coins, and left as discreetly as he could.

**

Now the success of Benk's dealings in meat relied on clandestine cooperation with the foreigners. In other words - bribes.

The meat had to come from somewhere and the only sources were the hunting parties who ventured out, often to the uncivilised north, under the protection of a few soldiers.

Benk was well-in with one such group which operated under the leadership of a Roman general who enjoyed hunting, and went by the name of Tertius.

And so the next day Benk called on Tertius and slid him two of his precious coins for future services. Tertius's other love was for money. So he thanked Benk and slid the coins into his belt purse and rushed off to join the hunt which was anxious to make the most of the day.

But for Tertius it was to prove to be a very bad day indeed.

The hunters had cornered a large boar. This animal had taken shelter in a small cave. It was stalemate with the group unable to prise the boar out, and the boar unable to escape.

Eventually Tertius's impatience overcame his common sense.

Grabbing a spear from one of the men, he crouched down and charged into the cave.

Unfortunately he found there wasn't space enough to wield the weapon with any degree of force, and he only succeeded in wounding the boar. A frightened, cornered, and wounded boar is a terrible thing, and this one was no exception. It hurled itself at Tertius and sank its teeth into his neck.

Tertius died, and the animal sought its freedom only to be savaged by the waiting hunters.

The first to reach Tertius was one Wallind. In the cave and out of sight of the others Wallind spotted Tertius's purse and in a flash removed the two coins and hid them in his shoe.

Stretchers were assembled for both Tertius and the boar and they were carried unceremoniously back to the Roman camp.

Later Tertius's body was buried with due ceremony in sight of the wall.

***

Tillus Maximus was tax collector for Arius Augustus, and was starting off on his way to his first call. The evening was cloudy and close with thunder rumbling ever closer. Tillus cursed the weather, the country, the heathens who lived there, and his job.

The coins were burning a hole in Wallind's shoe, he knew full well the penalty if he should be caught with them.

Unfortumately for Wallind his easy living was about to catch up with him.

He had just arrived at his home which was, thanks to his good connections, somewhat better than most; when Tillus Maximus arrived. Tillus usually demanded and got payment in kind, and in his obsequious way asked Wallind what he was offering by way of payment today, pointing out that tax was already due for two periods.

Wallind had no desire to part with anything, and suddenly remembered the two coins still secreted in his shoe.

Ah well, he thought, the coins were easily come by and he knew that money would be much preferred over goods. So out of sight of Tillus he removed the coins, replaced his shoe and returned with them in his hand.

Tillus had been collecting taxes for a very long time and knew better than to ask questions about how Willand had come by them. So without a word he took the coins, placed them carefully in his belt pouch, and taking a chalk entered the transaction on the tablet hung at his waist.

Then with no thanks or acknowledgement Tillus turned and set of for his next encounter.

He didn't get very far.

Struggling up a steep rise he was blinded by an immense flash of lightening which seared the ground no more than one hundred paces away. Tillus dropped to the ground stunned but not dead.

He was discovered by a guard troop as they marched their section of the Big Wall. They were well disciplined, took Tillus to the camp surgeon where he recovered in due course, and they formally took charge of the purse and the tablet.

The very next day the sergeant of the guard presented himself to Arius Augustus and handed over the Tax collector's purse and tablet, for which he was duly thanked.

When the soldier had left Arius glanced at he tablet, shrugged his shoulders at the small amount, and pocketed the contents of the purse.

He had, of course, no idea that these were the very same two coins with which he had obtained the favours of Sten just a few short days go.

JML
15/3/2007

ISBN 1425143008